I0687849

BOUND BY DANGER

ISBN-13:
979-8-9927180-0-3

Author's Note

Thank you for picking up Bound By Danger and giving it a read! If you enjoy this book as much as I hope you will, please leave a review or any feedback. Thanks again!

S. S. Bone

This book is dedicated to my husband, my children, and my book besties!!! Thank you for allowing me to write. Thank you for supporting me on this crazy journey. Thank you for letting me bounce ideas off you. I truly appreciate everything. Much love.

Table of Contents

Chapter One

Emily Blake navigated through the dense crowds of New York City with the practiced ease of someone who had spent most of her life weaving through its chaos. The city was a living, breathing organism— noisy, relentless, and unapologetically alive. Neon lights flickered above, casting a kaleidoscope of colors on the wet pavement. Car horns blared, and the scent of street food mingled with the faint, lingering smell of rain. To Emily, it was home.

Her life as a private investigator and hacker had led her down many dark alleys, both literal and metaphorical. Tonight, her target was a seemingly legitimate company suspected of being a front for mafia activities. The client was anonymous, the pay was substantial, and the risks were high—just the way Emily liked it.

Emily had been hired to investigate Tiberius Industries, a company with an impeccable facade. Their portfolio boasted everything from real estate to technology investments. But beneath the polished veneer, rumors of money laundering and illegal arms deals swirled. Her task was to gather concrete evidence to bring the truth to light.

She had spent the last week piecing together the company's structure, finding links that led to one name repeatedly: Dominic Valenti. He was the leader of one of the most feared mafia families in the city. Known for his ruthlessness and strategic mind, he was a man no one dared to cross. Emily had always enjoyed a challenge, and Dominic Valenti was the epitome of one.

Her latest lead pointed her to Luxe, a high-end club in the heart of Manhattan, frequented by the elite and infamous. The club was known for its exclusivity, its opulence, and the whispered conversations that held secrets worth millions. Emily had managed to secure a spot on the guest list using her skills to create a digital ghost—a persona convincing enough to bypass even the most stringent security checks.

As she stepped into the club, she was immediately struck by the ambiance. Crystal chandeliers cast a soft glow over the velvet-covered walls, and the air was thick with the scent of expensive perfume and aged whiskey. The patrons, dressed in designer clothing, sipped on their drinks, engaged in hushed conversations. Emily's eyes scanned the room, looking for her target.

She spotted him near the back, in a private booth surrounded by bodyguards. Dominic Valenti was everything the rumors had suggested and more. Tall and imposing, with dark, slicked-back hair and a chiseled jawline, he exuded power and confidence. His suit was tailored to perfection, and his eyes—sharp and calculating—scanned the room with a predator's awareness.

Emily felt a jolt of something unfamiliar. It wasn't fear, though any sane person would feel a twinge of it in his presence. It was an undeniable, magnetic attraction. She shook it off, focusing on her mission. Her goal was to get close enough to plant a device that would allow her to monitor his conversations.

She approached the bar and ordered a drink, positioning herself to get a better view of Dominic. As she sipped her cocktail, she felt a presence beside her. Turning slightly, she saw Dominic had left his booth and was now standing next to her.

"Enjoying the evening?" His voice was smooth, with a hint of an Italian accent, and it sent a shiver down her spine.

Emily met his gaze, her own eyes steady and unwavering. "I am now."

A faint smile tugged at the corner of his mouth. "I don't think we've met before. I'm Dominic."

"Emily," she replied, keeping her tone casual. "Just in town for a bit. Thought I'd check out the local scene."

His eyes narrowed slightly, as if trying to read between the lines of her simple statement. "The local scene can be...interesting. What brings you to Luxe?"

"Curiosity," she said with a shrug. "I hear it's the place to be."

Dominic's smile widened, but it didn't reach his eyes. "Curiosity can be dangerous."

Emily tilted her head slightly, mirroring his smile. "Only if you're not careful."

The tension between them crackled like electricity. Dominic's bodyguards watched from

Dominic's gaze was intense, as if he could see through her facade. "Indeed. Security is paramount, especially in my line of work."

Emily's heart raced, but she kept her expression neutral. "And what line of work is that?"

He smiled again, a predator's smile. "Let's just say I manage a variety of interests."

Before she could respond, a commotion at the entrance drew their attention. A group of men, clearly not on the guest list, had forced their way in, and the atmosphere shifted from relaxed to tense in an instant. Dominic's bodyguards moved swiftly, positioning themselves between the intruders and their boss.

Dominic turned back to Emily, his expression now deadly serious. "Stay here."

The club erupted into chaos. Shouts and curses filled the air as the intruders clashed with the security team. Emily watched as Dominic moved with lethal grace, taking down one of the men with a single, well-placed punch. She had no doubt he could handle himself, but she wasn't about to be a sitting duck.

She reached into her bag, pulling out a small, discreet device. If she couldn't plant it on Dominic directly, she could at least get it close enough to pick up his conversations. She slipped it under the bar, ensuring it was well-hidden.

The fight didn't last long. Dominic and his men quickly overpowered the intruders, dragging them out of the club. The patrons, some visibly shaken, others seemingly unfazed, resumed their activities as if nothing had happened. Dominic returned to Emily, his suit slightly rumpled but otherwise unscathed.

"Sorry about that," he said, adjusting his cuffs. "Business can be unpredictable."

Emily gave a small smile. "It certainly keeps things interesting."

Dominic looked at her with renewed interest. "You handled that well. Most people would have run for the exit."

"I've seen my share of excitement," she replied nonchalantly. "It takes a lot to rattle me."

Dominic's eyes lingered on her for a moment longer before he nodded. "I can see that. Perhaps we should continue this conversation somewhere less...chaotic."

Emily's heart skipped a beat. The rational part of her mind screamed caution, but the part of her that thrived on danger was tempted. Very tempted.

"I'll think about it," she said, her tone light. "But for now, I should be going."

Dominic didn't press her. He simply nodded, a knowing look in his eyes. "I look forward to our paths crossing again, Emily."

As she left the club, Emily couldn't shake the feeling that this encounter had set off a chain of events that would change everything. The tension, the attraction, and the danger were all intertwined in a way that was as exhilarating as it was terrifying. She knew one thing for certain—Dominic Valenti was a man who would not easily be forgotten.

Chapter Two

Emily waited until well past midnight before making her move. The office building housing Tiberius Industries was a fortress of modern security, with guards patrolling the perimeter and a state-of-the-art alarm system. But Emily was no ordinary intruder; she was a skilled hacker with a knack for bypassing even the most sophisticated defenses.

Clad in black, Emily walked swiftly through the city's darkened streets, her thoughts racing. The confrontation with Dominic had been intense, but she had managed to keep her cool. She needed to get back to her safe house, reassess her plans, and decide her next move.

As she navigated the labyrinth of alleyways and backstreets, she couldn't shake the feeling that Dominic's eyes were still on her. He was a formidable opponent, and she had no doubt that he would be watching her every move from now on.

She finally reached her safe house, a nondescript apartment in a quiet part of town. Inside, she secured the locks and set up her surveillance equipment, ensuring she wasn't followed. The room was filled with computer monitors and other tech, the tools of her trade. She sat down at her desk, taking a deep breath before powering up her systems.

Emily plugged in the flash drive she had managed to lift from Dominic's office—a small victory in an otherwise perilous night. She began to sift through the files, her fingers flying over the keyboard.
Most of the data was encrypted, but she had the skills to crack it.

As she worked, she couldn't help but replay the encounter in her mind. Dominic Valenti was unlike anyone she had ever met. His presence was overwhelming, his intelligence and cunning evident in every word and action. And yet, there had been a moment—just a flicker— when she had seen something else in his eyes. Curiosity, perhaps? Or something deeper?

The files finally decrypted, revealing a trove of information. Financial records, transaction logs, and communication transcripts—all pointing to the illegal activities she had suspected. Money laundering, arms deals, and more. This was exactly what she needed.

But as she delved deeper, she found something unexpected. A series of emails between Dominic and a mysterious figure known only as "The Broker." These communications hinted at a larger, more dangerous game being played—

one that involved not just Dominic's empire, but other powerful entities as well.

Emily knew she had to tread carefully. The information she had uncovered was explosive, but it also put her in greater danger. Dominic would not take kindly to her prying into his affairs, and The Broker—whoever they were— would be even more ruthless.

She backed up the files, encrypting them with multiple layers of security. Then she began to formulate her next steps. She needed to find out more about 'The Broker' and their connection to Dominic. But more importantly, she needed to stay one step ahead of them both.

As she worked, her phone buzzed. It was a message from her best friend and occasional partner, Jess.

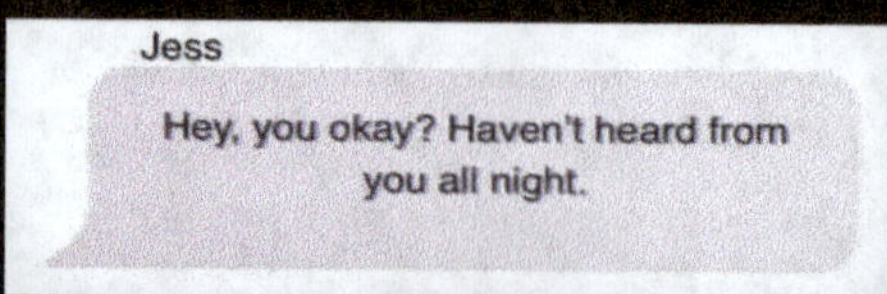

Jess was already there, sipping on a latte. She looked up as Emily approached, her eyes widening in concern.

"You look like you've had quite a night," Jess said, motioning for Emily to sit.

"You have no idea," Emily replied, sliding into the seat across from her. She quickly recounted the events of the previous night, from the break in, to the confrontation with Dominic.

Jess listened intently, her expression shifting from concern to amazement. "You went toe-to-toe with Dominic Valenti and lived to tell the tale? Damn, Emily. That's impressive."

Emily shrugged. "It's not over yet. I got the evidence we need, but I also uncovered something bigger. Have you ever heard of someone called 'The Broker'?"

Jess's eyes widened. "'The Broker'? Yeah, I've heard whispers. They're supposedly one of the most connected people in the underworld, dealing in information, weapons, you name it. If they're involved, this is bigger than we thought."

Emily nodded. "Exactly. We need to find out more about 'The Broker' and their connection to Dominic. And we need to be careful. If they realize we're onto them, we could be in serious danger."

Jess leaned back in her chair, her mind clearly racing. "We'll need to dig deep, but we can do it. What's the plan?"

"We start by tracing the emails I found," Emily said. "There's got to be a way to track down The Broker. And we need to keep a low profile. Dominic's already suspicious, and we can't afford any mistakes."

Jess nodded, a determined look in her eyes. "Alright. Let's do this."

The next few days were a whirlwind of activity. Emily and Jess worked tirelessly, tracing the emails and following leads. They uncovered a network of shell companies and offshore accounts, all linked back to The Broker. It was a tangled web, but they were slowly making progress.

One evening, as Emily sat at her desk, her phone buzzed with an incoming call. The number was unlisted, but she answered it cautiously.

"Hello?"

"Emily Blake." Dominic's voice was unmistakable, sending a jolt of adrenaline through her.

"Dominic," she replied, keeping her voice steady. "To what do I owe the pleasure?"

"I've been thinking about our little encounter," he said smoothly. "And I find myself...intrigued. You're not like anyone I've ever met."

Emily's heart raced, but she forced herself to remain calm. "Is that so?"

"Yes," he continued. "And I believe we might have more to discuss. In person. Tomorrow night, Luxe. Don't be late."

Before she could respond, the line went dead.

Emily stared at the phone, her mind racing. Dominic wanted to meet again. This could be an opportunity to learn more, but it was also incredibly dangerous. She knew she had to be careful, but she couldn't pass up the chance.

The next night, Emily found herself back at Luxe. The club was just as opulent and exclusive as before, but this time, she felt the weight of Dominic's gaze the moment she walked in.

He was waiting for her in the same private booth, his expression unreadable. As she approached, he motioned for her to sit.

"Emily," he said, his voice smooth. "I'm glad you decided to join me."

"I was curious," she replied, taking a seat. "What's this about, Dominic?"

He leaned back, studying her. "I've been thinking about you. About your skills. And I have a proposition for you."

Emily's heart pounded, but she kept her expression neutral. "I'm listening."

"I have a problem that needs solving," he said, his eyes locking onto hers. "And I think you're the perfect person to handle it."

She raised an eyebrow. "And what makes you think I'd help you?"

"Because you're curious," he replied with a faint smile. "And because I can make it worth your while."

Emily considered his words carefully. This could be a trap, but it could also be an opportunity to get closer to Dominic and uncover more about his operations.

"Alright," she said finally. "I'll hear you out."

Dominic's smile widened, a glint of satisfaction in his eyes. "Good. Let's get started."

As they began to discuss the details of his proposition, Emily couldn't help but feel a thrill of anticipation. The game was getting more dangerous, but it was also becoming more intriguing. She had to be careful, but she was determined to see this through—no matter where it led.

And as Dominic spoke, she couldn't shake the feeling that their paths were becoming increasingly intertwined, each step drawing them closer to a collision that would change everything.

Chapter Three

The early morning light filtered through the blinds of Emily's apartment, casting long shadows across her cluttered desk. The evidence she had gathered so far lay spread out before her: encrypted files, photos, transaction records, and a tangled web of connections that all pointed to Dominic Valenti. She sipped her coffee, her mind working through the maze of information.

Emily knew that to bring Dominic down, she had to uncover every detail of his operations. The flash drive from his office had been a goldmine, but it was just the beginning. She needed more—more evidence, more leverage. And she needed to stay one step ahead of

Dominic and his men, who were undoubtedly already on her trail.

She set up a secure connection to her server and began hacking into the shell companies and offshore accounts linked to Dominic. Each click of her keyboard brought her closer to the heart of his empire. She could almost feel the walls closing in around him.

As she worked, Emily's thoughts drifted back to her past, to the events that had shaped her into the person she was today. She had always been good with computers, a talent that had set her apart from her peers. But it wasn't until college that she discovered her true calling.

She had been a freshman, studying computer science, when her best friend, Sarah, disappeared. The police had been useless, treating her friend's case as just another runaway. But Emily had known better. She had hacked into school records, traced phone calls, and pieced together the clues that led her to a human trafficking ring operating right under their noses. With the evidence she had gathered, the police had been forced to act, and Sarah had been rescued.

That experience had changed Emily. It had shown her the power of information, the importance of justice, and the thrill of outsmarting those who thought they were untouchable. She had switched her major to criminal justice, learning everything she could about investigation and law. After graduating, she had started her own private investigation firm, using her skills to help those who had nowhere else to turn.

Her current case was personal in a way few others had been. The anonymous client had paid well, but the real motivation was her sense of justice. Dominic Valenti was a blight on the city, his power and influence corrupting everything he touched. Emily wanted to bring him down, not just for her client, but for herself and for all the people he had hurt.

Emily's focus sharpened as she uncovered more about Dominic's operations. She traced the flow of money through a labyrinth of shell companies, each one a piece of the puzzle. The transactions pointed to bribes, illicit deals, and connections with other criminal organizations. The picture was becoming clearer, but she knew she had only scratched the surface.

She was so engrossed in her work that she didn't notice the black SUV parked across the street from her apartment. Inside, two of Dominic's men watched her building, their eyes never straying from the front door.

"She's been in there all morning," one of them said, lowering his binoculars. "Boss wants us to keep an eye on her."

The other man nodded, his gaze fixed on the entrance. "She's good. Too good. Boss thinks she's a threat."

Back in her apartment, Emily's phone buzzed, pulling her from her thoughts. It was a message from Jess.

* * *

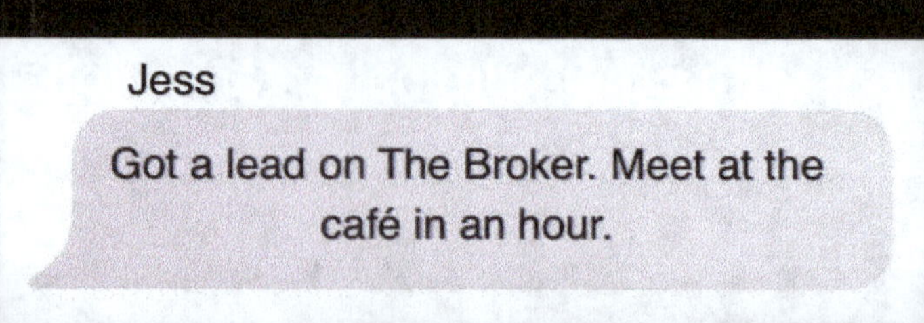

Emily quickly replied.

She gathered her things, making sure to secure her laptop and files. As she stepped out onto the street, she felt a prickle of unease. She scanned the area, her instincts alerting her to the possibility of surveillance. She spotted the black SUV, the men inside watching her intently. She had been expecting this, and she was prepared.

Emily took a circuitous route to the café, weaving through alleys and side streets to shake any potential tails. By the time she arrived, she was confident she hadn't been followed. Jess was already there, her laptop open and a coffee steaming in front of her.

"Hey," Jess said, looking up as Emily slid into the seat across from her. "I've been digging into The Broker. It's not much, but I found a few things."

Emily leaned in, eager to hear what Jess had uncovered. "What did you find?"

Jess turned her laptop around to show a series of documents and photos. "The Broker is a ghost. No real name, no solid identity. But there are rumors and whispers. They deal in information, arms, and other illegal trades. And they have connections all over the world. From what I can gather, they're involved in some kind of high-stakes deal with Dominic."

* * *

Emily's mind raced as she processed the information. "If we can find out what that deal is, we might have enough to bring them both down."

Jess nodded. "I also found this." She clicked on a file, bringing up a map with several locations marked. "These are properties linked to Dominic. One of them is a warehouse in the industrial district. It's heavily guarded, but if The Broker is involved, there's a good chance something important is happening there."

Emily studied the map, her determination solidifying. "We need to get inside that warehouse. It could be the key to everything."

The two women spent the next hour planning their approach. They would need to be careful, gathering intel and formulating a strategy to infiltrate the warehouse. Emily knew it would be dangerous, but the potential payoff was too great to ignore.

As they finalized their plans, Emily couldn't shake the feeling of being watched. She glanced out the window, her eyes scanning the street. She didn't see the SUV, but she knew Dominic's men were out there, keeping tabs on her.

"We need to be extra careful," Emily said, turning back to Jess. "Dominic's men are watching me. They're not going to make this easy."

Jess nodded, her expression serious. "We'll get in and out quickly. No mistakes."

Over the next few days, Emily and Jess kept a low profile, avoiding any actions that might tip off Dominic's men. They gathered intel on the warehouse, noting the guards' routines and the security measures in place. Each piece of information brought them closer to their goal.

Emily's nights were spent poring over the files she had gathered, looking for any additional clues. She learned more about Dominic's empire, his connections, and his ruthlessness. The more she uncovered, the more determined she became to see him brought to justice.

But Dominic wasn't idle. His men continued to watch her, reporting back to him with every move she made. Dominic listened to their reports, a mixture of curiosity and frustration gnawing at him. Emily Blake was proving to be a formidable opponent, one who intrigued him even as she threatened his operations.

One evening, as Dominic sat in his office, his top lieutenant, Matteo, entered with an update.

"Boss, she's been quiet," Matteo said. "No sign of her making any big moves. But she's definitely digging. We need to act before she finds something we can't cover up."

Dominic leaned back in his chair, his mind working through the possibilities. "Keep watching her. But don't make a move yet. I want to see what she does next."

Matteo nodded, leaving Dominic alone with his thoughts. Dominic's eyes narrowed as he considered Emily. She was smart, resourceful, and relentless. A dangerous combination, but also one that fascinated him. He wondered what drove her, what secrets lay behind those determined eyes.

The night of the infiltration came quickly. Emily and Jess were ready, their plan meticulously crafted. They dressed in black, their gear packed and ready. As they approached the warehouse, they kept to the shadows, avoiding the guards and security cameras.

They reached a side entrance, Jess working quickly to disable the alarm while Emily kept watch. Once inside, they moved silently through the dimly lit corridors, their senses on high alert. The warehouse was a labyrinth of crates and machinery, the air thick with the scent of oil and metal.

They found a secure room at the heart of the warehouse, the door heavily guarded. Emily's heart raced as they prepared to breach it. This was it—the moment of truth.

Jess used a small device to disable the electronic lock, and the door clicked open. They slipped inside, finding themselves in a room filled with documents, computer terminals, and stacks of cash. At the center was a large table, a detailed map of the city spread out across it, marked with various points of interest.

Emily's eyes widened as she recognized the significance. This was the nerve center of Dominic's operations. She moved quickly, photographing the documents and copying the data from the computers. Every second counted.

Just as they were finishing, the sound of footsteps echoed down the corridor. Emily's heart pounded as she signaled Jess. They had to move, and fast.

They slipped out of the room, retracing their steps through the warehouse. The footsteps grew louder, the guards closing in. They ducked into a side passage, holding their breath as the guards passed by.

Once the coast was clear, they made their way to the exit, their hearts racing with the thrill of the escape. They had done it. They had the evidence they needed.

Back at her apartment, Emily and Jess reviewed their haul. The data confirmed everything they had suspected: Dominic's ties to The Broker, the illegal deals, and the bribes. It was enough to bring down his entire operation.

But as they poured over the information, Emily's phone buzzed. She glanced at the screen and saw an unknown number. With a nod to Jess, she answered, her voice steady.

"Hello?"

"Emily Blake," came Dominic's smooth voice. "I must commend you on your skills. It's not often someone gets this far. But you've made a mistake."

Emily's heart skipped a beat, but she kept her voice calm. "And what mistake would that be?"

"Underestimating me," Dominic replied. "You see, while you've been busy digging into my affairs, I've been learning about you. I know where you live. I know who your friends are. And I know what drives you."

Emily's grip tightened on the phone. "If you think you can scare me—"

"I don't need to scare you," Dominic interrupted. "I just need to offer you a choice. You have something I want. And I have something you want."

Emily's mind raced. What could Dominic possibly offer her? "I'm listening."

"I propose a meeting," Dominic said. "A truce, if you will. We discuss our respective interests and find a mutually beneficial solution."

Emily glanced at Jess, who was listening intently. She knew this was a dangerous game, but she also knew that meeting Dominic could give her the leverage she needed. "Where and when?"

"Tomorrow night, Luxe," Dominic said. "Same place as before. Don't be late."

The line went dead, leaving Emily to stare at her phone. She looked at Jess, her mind already working through the implications.

"We need to be careful," Jess said. "This could be a trap."

"I know," Emily replied. "But it's a risk we have to take. We need to find out what Dominic's real game is."

The next day was a blur of preparation. Emily and Jess went over their plan again and again, making sure they had contingencies for every possible scenario. They secured the evidence they had gathered, ensuring it was safe in case something went wrong.

Emily dressed carefully for the meeting, opting for an outfit that was both professional and practical. She needed to project confidence and control, even as she walked into the lion's den. She concealed a small recording device in her jacket, ready to capture every word of their conversation.

As the evening approached, Emily couldn't shake the feeling of anticipation. She knew this meeting could change everything. It was a chance to get closer to Dominic, to understand his motivations, and perhaps to find a way to take him down once and for all.

Luxe was as opulent as ever, its gleaming marble floors and crystal chandeliers casting a glittering reflection. Emily walked through the entrance, her eyes scanning the room for any signs of danger. She spotted Dominic in the same private booth, his expression unreadable.

"Emily," he greeted her as she approached. "I'm glad you decided to join me."

"I'm here to listen," she replied, taking a seat across from him. "What's this all about?"

Dominic leaned back, his eyes studying her intently. "You've proven yourself to be quite resourceful. I admire that. But you've also become a problem. One that needs solving."

Emily kept her expression neutral. "And you think you can solve it by talking?"

"I think we can find a way to coexist," Dominic said. "You see, I'm not just a criminal. I'm a businessman. And I recognize talent when I see it. You have skills that could be very useful to me."

Emily raised an eyebrow. "You're offering me a job?"

"Not just a job," Dominic replied. "A partnership. You help me with a certain problem, and in return, I make sure you and your friends are safe. And you get a share of the profits."

Emily's mind raced. This was unexpected. A partnership with Dominic Valenti? It was a tempting offer, but she knew it was a double-edged sword. "What kind of problem?"

"The Broker," Dominic said, his tone serious. "They're becoming a liability. I need someone who can help me neutralize that threat. Someone who knows how to dig deep and uncover the truth."

Emily considered his words carefully. This could be the leverage she needed. "And what's to stop you from turning on me once The Broker is dealt with?"

"A fair question," Dominic replied. "I suppose you'll just have to trust me."

Emily let out a soft laugh. "Trust you? That's a tall order."

"I know," Dominic said, his eyes locking onto hers. "But consider the alternative. You continue your crusade, and you put yourself and everyone you care about in danger. Or we work together, and we both get what we want."

Emily leaned back, her mind working through the possibilities. She needed more time, more information. "I'll think about it," she said finally. "But I need something from you first."

Dominic raised an eyebrow. "And what would that be?"

"Proof that you're serious," Emily replied. "Information on The Broker. Something concrete."

Dominic nodded slowly. "Very well. I'll have my people send you a dossier. Consider it a gesture of good faith."

Emily stood, feeling the weight of his gaze on her. "I'll be in touch."

As she left Luxe, Emily couldn't shake the feeling of being watched. She knew Dominic's men were out there, tracking her every move. She made her way back to her apartment, her mind racing with the implications of Dominic's offer.

When she arrived home, she found Jess waiting, her expression tense.
"How did it go?"

* * *

Emily recounted the conversation, watching as Jess's eyes widened in surprise. "He wants to partner with you? That's... unexpected."

"I know," Emily replied. "But it could be the break we need. If we can use this to get closer to The Broker, we might be able to bring them both down."

Jess nodded, her determination matching Emily's. "We'll need to be careful. Dominic's playing a dangerous game."

"We always are," Emily said with a faint smile. "But we're getting closer. We just need to stay one step ahead."

The next morning, Emily received an encrypted email from an unknown sender. Attached was a dossier on The Broker, just as Dominic had promised. She opened it carefully, her heart pounding with anticipation.

The dossier contained detailed information on The Broker's operations, their known associates, and their dealings with Dominic. It was more than she had hoped for, a treasure trove of information that could help her unravel the web of corruption and crime.

But it also raised new questions. The Broker was more powerful and connected than she had realized. Taking them down would be a monumental task, one that would require all of her skills and resources.

As she poured over the dossier, Emily couldn't shake the feeling that she was on the brink of something big. The pieces were falling into place, but the game was far from over. She knew she had to be careful, to navigate the dangerous waters she found herself in.

But one thing was certain: she was closer than ever to the truth. And she wouldn't stop until she had brought Dominic and The Broker to justice.

Emily leaned back in her chair, her mind racing with possibilities. The investigation was heating up, the stakes higher than ever. But she was ready. With Jess by her side and the evidence they had gathered, she knew they had a chance to take down Dominic Valenti and The Broker.

As she prepared for the next phase of their plan, Emily couldn't help but feel a thrill of anticipation. The game was dangerous, but it was also exhilarating. And she was determined to win.

With a deep breath, she turned back to her computer, ready to dive deeper into the investigation. The truth was out there, and she would find it—no matter what it took.

Chapter Four

Emily's office was dimly lit, the soft glow of her computer screen casting shadows on the walls. She had been working tirelessly, combing through the dossier Dominic had provided. The information was dense, filled with cryptic references and coded messages. But Emily had a knack for unraveling puzzles, and she was determined to find the piece that would blow the whole case wide open.

Her breakthrough came late in the evening. As she sifted through financial records and transaction logs, she noticed a series of payments that stood out. They were routed through multiple shell companies, making them difficult to trace. But Emily recognized the pattern—she had seen it before in cases involving money laundering.

She leaned in closer, her eyes scanning the screen. The payments were tied to a legitimate business owned by Dominic, a high-end logistics company. On the surface, it appeared to be a reputable enterprise. But the financial records told a different story. Large sums of money were being funneled through the company and then disappearing into offshore accounts.

Emily's heart raced as she connected the dots. This was it—the link she needed to tie Dominic's business to illegal activities. She quickly began compiling the evidence, taking screenshots and noting down critical information. This was the smoking gun that could bring Dominic down.

Just as Emily finished compiling her evidence, she heard the sound of footsteps in the hallway outside her office. Her body tensed, and she quickly saved her work, closing her laptop. She stood, ready to face whoever was approaching.

The door burst open, and Dominic strode in, his eyes blazing with anger. He was dressed impeccably, as always, but there was a dangerous edge to his demeanor.

"Emily," he said, his voice low and menacing. "We need to talk."

Emily stood her ground, her heart pounding. "I'm busy, Dominic. What do you want?"

He stepped closer, his presence overwhelming. "I warned you to stay out of my business. But you just couldn't help yourself, could you?"

She crossed her arms, refusing to back down. "I'm doing my job. And it looks like I've uncovered something you didn't want me to find."

Dominic's eyes narrowed. "You have no idea what you're dealing with."

"Oh, I think I do," Emily shot back. "Your logistics company is a front for money laundering. I have the proof."

Dominic's jaw clenched, and for a moment, Emily thought he might lash out. But instead, he took a deep breath, reigning in his anger. "You're playing a dangerous game, Emily."

"I'm not the one breaking the law," she replied, her voice steady. "You are. And I'm going to make sure you pay for it."

There was a tense silence, the air between them crackling with unresolved tension. Dominic's eyes bore into hers, and she could feel the intensity of his emotions. Anger, frustration, but also something else— something that made her pulse quicken.

"You're making a mistake," he said finally, his voice softer but no less intense. "You think you're untouchable because you're smart and resourceful. But you're wrong. There are consequences to your actions."

Emily met his gaze, refusing to be intimidated. "I know the risks. And I'm willing to take them."

Dominic stepped even closer, his face inches from hers. She could feel the heat radiating from his body, and her breath caught in her throat. Despite the danger, despite the anger, there was an undeniable attraction between them.

"You're too stubborn for your own good," he murmured, his voice low and rough. "But I can't say I don't admire that."

Emily's heart pounded in her chest. She could feel the tension between them, the magnetic pull that she couldn't deny. She hated herself for it, but she couldn't help the way her body reacted to his presence.

"Stay out of my business," Dominic warned, his eyes burning into hers. "This is your last chance."

Emily swallowed hard, forcing herself to stay strong. "Or what? You'll kill me?"

Dominic's expression softened slightly, a flicker of something almost like regret crossing his face. "I don't want to hurt you, Emily. But I will if I have to."

They stood there, locked in a battle of wills, neither willing to back down. The room was filled with the intensity of their emotions, the charged atmosphere almost suffocating. Emily could feel her resolve wavering, the conflicting emotions tearing at her.

Finally, Dominic took a step back, his expression hardening once more. "This is your last warning. Stay out of my business, or there will be consequences."

With that, he turned and strode out of the office, leaving Emily standing there, her mind reeling. She took a deep breath, trying to steady herself. The confrontation had left her shaken, but also more determined than ever.

* * *

She knew the risks. She knew that going up against Dominic Valenti was dangerous. But she couldn't back down now. She had come too far, uncovered too much. She had to see this through to the end.

As she sat back down at her desk, Emily's mind raced with plans and strategies. She needed to be careful, to stay one step ahead of Dominic and his men. But she also needed to use the evidence she had gathered to bring him to justice.

The stakes were higher than ever, and the game was far from over. But Emily was ready. She would face whatever came her way, no matter the cost.

She opened her laptop and resumed her work, her resolve stronger than ever. Dominic's warning echoed in her mind, but she pushed it aside. She had a job to do, and she wouldn't stop until it was done.

As she delved deeper into the investigation, Emily couldn't help but feel a thrill of anticipation. The confrontation with Dominic had only fueled her determination. She was on the brink of something big, and she wouldn't let anything—or anyone—stand in her way.

But even as she worked, a part of her couldn't forget the intensity of Dominic's gaze, the underlying attraction that simmered between them. It was a distraction she couldn't afford, but one that she couldn't entirely shake.

With a deep breath, Emily pushed those thoughts aside and focused on the task at hand. The truth was out there, and she would find it—no matter what it took. The game was on, and she was ready to play.

Emily's discovery had set the stage for a high-stakes battle, one that would test her skills and determination like never before. She knew the road ahead would be dangerous, filled with risks and challenges. But she was ready to face it head-on.

With the evidence she had uncovered, she was closer than ever to bringing Dominic Valenti and his empire to justice. But she also knew that the confrontation with Dominic was just the beginning. There were still many pieces of the puzzle to uncover, many obstacles to overcome.

As she delved deeper into the investigation, Emily steeled herself for what lay ahead. The stakes were higher than ever, but she was ready. She had come too far to turn back now.

And no matter what Dominic threw at her, she wouldn't stop until she had brought him to justice. The game was dangerous, but it was one she was determined to win.

Chapter Five

The sunlight streamed through the windows of Emily's modest apartment, casting long shadows across her makeshift office space. Piles of documents, photographs, and notes were spread across her desk, all connected by a web of red string and push pins on the cork board behind her. She sipped her coffee, its warmth a small comfort against the growing chill of tension that had settled in her bones since Dominic's warning.

She couldn't let Dominic's intimidation tactics deter her. She was too close to the truth, and her resolve had only hardened. As she dug deeper into the logistics company's records, she found more evidence of money laundering and illegal shipments, all carefully hidden behind layers of legitimate business transactions.

Emily's phone buzzed on the desk, breaking her concentration. She glanced at the screen and saw Jess's name. She picked up, grateful for the brief distraction.

"Hey, Jess," Emily greeted her friend, trying to sound more relaxed than she felt.

"Emily, we need to talk," Jess's voice was tight with worry. "I heard about your run-in with Dominic. You need to be careful. This guy is dangerous."

Emily sighed, leaning back in her chair. "I know, Jess. But I can't stop now. I'm so close to uncovering everything."

* * *

"I get it, but Dominic's not someone to mess with lightly. He has a reputation, and if he's threatened, he'll retaliate. Promise me you'll be careful."

"I promise," Emily said, though she wasn't sure how much she meant it. "I'll watch my back."

"Good," Jess replied, the tension in her voice easing slightly. "Just... don't do anything reckless, okay?"

"Okay," Emily agreed, ending the call and staring at her screen. She knew Jess was right, but she also knew she couldn't let fear stop her. She took a deep breath, steeling herself to dive back into her work.

Later that evening, Emily decided to step out for a breath of fresh air. She had been cooped up in her apartment for hours, and the walls felt like they were closing in on her. She threw on a jacket and headed out into the cool night air, her mind still buzzing with thoughts of the investigation.

As she walked through the quiet streets, she felt a sense of unease creeping up on her. The hairs on the back of her neck stood up, and she had the distinct feeling she was being watched. She quickened her pace, glancing over her shoulder, but saw nothing out of the ordinary.

Her phone buzzed in her pocket. She pulled it out and saw a text from an unknown number.

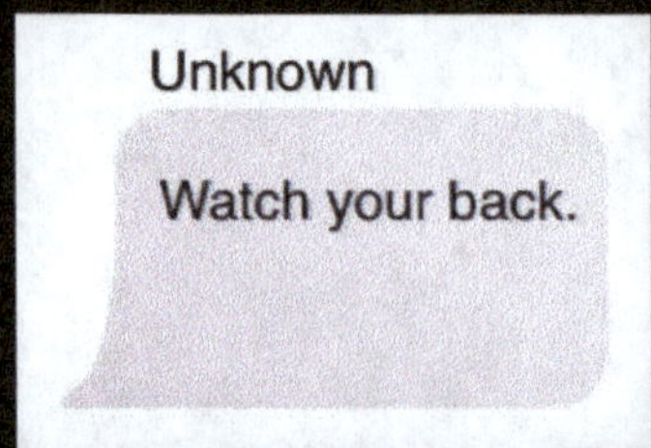

Her heart raced, and she picked up her pace, her eyes scanning her surroundings more carefully now.

She turned a corner and froze. A black SUV was parked at the end of the alley, its engine idling. She took a step back, but it was too late. Two men emerged from the shadows, their faces obscured by hoods.

"Miss Blake," one of them said, his voice cold and menacing. "We have a message for you."

Emily's mind raced. She had no time to think, only to act. She turned on her heel and sprinted back the way she came, her breath coming in ragged gasps. She heard the men behind her, their footsteps pounding on the pavement.

She darted down another alley, her heart pounding in her chest. The alley was a dead end. She was trapped. She turned to face her pursuers, her mind racing for a way out.

Just as the men closed in, a sleek black car screeched to a halt at the mouth of the alley. Dominic stepped out, his expression cold and furious. The men hesitated, clearly recognizing him.

"Get away from her," Dominic commanded, his voice low and dangerous. "Now."

The men exchanged a glance, then slowly backed away, retreating into the shadows. Dominic watched them go, then turned his attention to Emily. She was breathing hard, her eyes wide with shock and confusion.

"What the hell are you doing here?" Emily demanded, trying to regain her composure.

"I could ask you the same thing," Dominic replied, his eyes narrowing. "I told you to stay out of my business."

"And I told you I'm not backing down," Emily shot back, her fear giving way to anger. "Why did you save me?"

Dominic stepped closer, his presence overwhelming. "Because those men weren't mine. They're part of a rival group. And if they kill you, it complicates things for me."

Emily's breath hitched as he moved even closer, his face inches from hers. She could feel the heat radiating off him, the intensity of his gaze making her pulse race.

"You need to understand something, Emily," Dominic said, his voice low and intense. "This world you're stepping into is dangerous. You think you're untouchable because you're smart and resourceful. But you're not. You need to stop this before you get yourself killed."

Emily met his gaze, refusing to back down. "I can't stop, Dominic. I have to see this through."

"You're too stubborn for your own good," he muttered, but there was a flicker of something in his eyes—admiration, maybe. "But I can't let you get hurt."

Emily's heart pounded in her chest, the tension between them almost unbearable. She could feel the pull, the undeniable attraction that simmered beneath their heated exchange. She hated herself for it, but she couldn't deny it.

"You care about what happens to me?" she asked, her voice barely above a whisper.

Dominic's jaw clenched. "I care about keeping things under control. And right now, you're a variable I can't predict."

They stood there, locked in a battle of wills, the air charged with unspoken emotions. Emily could feel her resolve wavering, the conflicting feelings tearing at her. She wanted to push him away, to escape the intensity of his presence, but she also wanted to lean into it, to see where this dangerous attraction would lead.

Finally, Dominic stepped back, breaking the spell. "Go home, Emily. And stay out of trouble."

Without another word, he turned and walked back to his car, leaving Emily standing in the alley, her mind reeling. She took a deep breath, trying to steady herself. The encounter had left her shaken, but also more determined than ever.

* * *

She knew the risks. She knew that going up against Dominic Valenti was dangerous. But she couldn't back down now. She had come too far, uncovered too much. She had to see this through to the end.

As she made her way back to her apartment, Emily couldn't shake the feeling of Dominic's eyes on her, the intensity of their exchange still lingering in her mind. She knew she was walking a fine line, but she couldn't let fear stop her. She had to stay one step ahead, to use the evidence she had gathered to bring him to justice.

When she finally reached her apartment, she locked the door behind her and leaned against it, taking a moment to catch her breath. She replayed the encounter in her mind, the way Dominic had looked at her, the way his presence had affected her. She shook her head, trying to push those thoughts aside.

She had a job to do, and she couldn't afford any distractions. Not even Dominic Valenti.

Emily moved to her desk and opened her laptop, determined to dive back into her work. She knew the road ahead would be dangerous, filled with risks and challenges. But she was ready to face it head-on.

With a deep breath, she focused on the screen, her resolve stronger than ever. The investigation was heating up, and the stakes were higher than ever. But she was ready. She had come too far to turn back now.

And no matter what Dominic threw at her, she wouldn't stop until she had brought him to justice. The game was dangerous, but it was one she ready for it.

Chapter Six

Dominic Valenti sat in his opulent office, high above the bustling city, staring out at the glittering skyline. The events of the previous night replayed in his mind—the fear in Emily's eyes, the determination in her voice, and the undeniable attraction that simmered between them. He had saved her on impulse, driven by an instinct he didn't fully understand. But now, in the cold light of day, he realized something crucial: Emily Blake could be more than just a thorn in his side. She could be an asset.

Dominic's operations were vast and intricate, and lately, he had been dealing with a series of setbacks that suggested an insider was sabotaging him. He needed someone who could uncover the truth without raising suspicion. Emily's skills as a hacker and investigator made her the perfect candidate. She had proven her resourcefulness and tenacity, and if he could harness that, it would give him a significant advantage.

But convincing her to work with him would be another matter entirely.

Emily was back in her apartment, the chaos of her makeshift office surrounding her. The encounter with Dominic had left her rattled, but also more determined. She was deep into her research when her phone buzzed. She glanced at the screen and saw a message from an unknown number.

* * *

Emily raised an eyebrow. "Help each other? Last time we spoke, you told me to stay out of your business or else."

"I know," he admitted. "But circumstances have changed. There's a traitor within my ranks, someone who's been feeding information to my rivals and undermining my operations. I need to find out who it is, and I believe you can help me."

Emily was taken aback. "And why would I help you?"

"Because I can offer you something in return," Dominic said, his voice low and persuasive. "Protection. You've already seen what my enemies are capable of. They won't stop until they've taken you out of the equation. Work with me, and I'll ensure your safety."

* * *

She considered his words, her mind racing. The idea of working with Dominic was abhorrent, but the protection he offered was tempting.

She had been in danger since she started this investigation, and aligning with him, even temporarily, could provide the security she needed to continue her work.

"I don't trust you," she said finally.

"You don't have to trust me," Dominic replied. "But we have a common goal. Find the traitor, and we both get what we want."

Emily hesitated, weighing her options. It was a risky move, but if she could uncover the traitor, it would not only help Dominic but also give her more leverage against him. She could gather more evidence, find more cracks in his empire.

"Fine," she said, her voice firm. "I'll help you. But I'm not doing this for you. I'm doing it because it's the best way to protect myself and to bring down your operation."

A flicker of admiration crossed Dominic's face. "Agreed. Now, let's discuss how we're going to do this."

They spent the next hour outlining their plan. Dominic provided Emily with a list of his closest associates and key players within his organization. Each one was a potential suspect. Emily's task was to dig into their backgrounds, find any discrepancies, and uncover who was leaking information.

"Start with these three," Dominic instructed, sliding a piece of paper across the table. "They've had access to sensitive information recently, and their actions have been suspicious."

Emily took the list, scanning the names. "And what will you be doing while I investigate?"

"I'll be handling the internal security measures, tightening the circle, and monitoring their movements," Dominic replied. "We'll stay in close communication. Any findings, you report to me immediately."

* * *

Emily nodded, though she still felt a knot of unease in her stomach. "Fine. But remember, if I sense any double-crossing, this deal is off."

"Understood," Dominic said, a hint of a smile playing at the corners of his mouth. "I don't take betrayal lightly."

With the plan set, Emily stood to leave. Dominic reached out and caught her arm, his grip firm but not painful. She looked down at his hand, then up into his eyes.

"Be careful, Emily," he said softly. "This is dangerous territory."

She pulled her arm free, her expression steely. "I can handle myself."

As she walked out of the coffee shop, she couldn't shake the feeling that she had just made a deal with the devil. But if it brought her closer to the truth and gave her the edge she needed, it was a risk she was willing to take.

Back in her apartment, Emily dove into the task at hand. She began with the names Dominic had given her, using her hacking skills to dig into their personal and professional lives. The first name on the list was Matteo Santini, one of Dominic's top lieutenants. Matteo had been with Dominic for years, but recently, his behavior had raised red flags.

Emily accessed his financial records, communications, and travel history. She looked for anything that seemed out of the ordinary. After several hours of searching, she found a series of encrypted emails that piqued her interest. They were sent to an unknown recipient, and the content was heavily coded.

She began the painstaking process of decoding the messages, her fingers flying over the keyboard. It was slow work, but eventually, she managed to crack one of the codes. The email contained a list of shipment dates and locations, information that only someone with insider knowledge would have.

Her heart raced as she realized the significance of what she had found. Matteo was feeding information to someone outside the organization. She needed to find out who that person was and what their connection was to Dominic's rivals.

The second name on the list was Sofia Ruiz, Dominic's personal assistant. Sofia was fiercely loyal and had been by Dominic's side through numerous crises. Emily was skeptical about her involvement, but she couldn't afford to leave any stone unturned.

She hacked into Sofia's phone and email accounts, sifting through her messages and call logs. Most of it was mundane—scheduling meetings, arranging travel plans, and handling logistics for Dominic's operations. But one email thread stood out. It was a series of messages between Sofia and an unknown contact, discussing a "delivery" that needed to be handled discreetly.

Emily dug deeper, tracing the IP address of the unknown contact. It led her to a small, unremarkable office building in the city's industrial district. She noted the location, planning to investigate further.

The third name on the list was Vincent Mancini, a trusted enforcer and Dominic's right-hand man. Vincent was known for his ruthlessness and efficiency. Emily accessed his bank records and found several large, unexplained deposits in offshore accounts. The timing of the deposits coincided with key operations that had been compromised.

She cross-referenced the transactions with known associates of Dominic's rivals and found a connection. One of the accounts was linked to a shell company owned by a rival family. Vincent was receiving payments in exchange for information.

Armed with this new information, Emily knew she needed to meet with Dominic. She arranged to meet him in a secure location—a safe house he used for sensitive meetings. When she arrived, Dominic was already there, his expression tense.

"What did you find?" he asked, his voice clipped.

Emily laid out her findings, detailing the evidence against Matteo, Sofia, and Vincent. Dominic listened intently, his expression growing darker with each revelation.

* * *

"Matteo is definitely leaking information," Emily concluded. "Sofia is handling a discreet delivery that might be connected to the traitor. And Vincent is receiving payments from a rival family."

Dominic's jaw tightened. "I knew there was a leak, but I didn't realize it was this widespread. We need to act fast."

Emily nodded. "I can help you set a trap, catch them in the act. But we need to be careful. If they suspect anything, they could disappear."

Dominic's eyes met hers, a mixture of gratitude and something else— respect. "You've done good work, Emily. Better than I expected."

She felt a flicker of pride but quickly tamped it down. "I'm not doing this for your approval, Dominic. I want these people brought to justice."

"And they will be," he assured her. "Together, we'll expose them and ensure they pay for their betrayal."

The plan was set into motion quickly. Emily and Dominic devised a scheme to lure the traitors into revealing themselves. They staged a fake shipment, using false information that only the inner circle would know. Emily monitored the communications, waiting for the traitors to take the bait.

As expected, Matteo contacted his unknown recipient, passing along the details of the fake shipment. Sofia was tasked with arranging the delivery, and Vincent, as the enforcer, was to ensure everything went smoothly. All three were falling neatly into the roles Dominic and Emily had predicted, confirming their involvement.

Emily set up surveillance on the designated warehouse where the fake shipment was supposed to take place. She positioned herself in a nearby building, using her laptop to monitor the feeds from hidden cameras and microphones placed around the warehouse. Dominic's men were also in position, ready to move at a moment's notice.

As the time for the fake shipment approached, Emily's pulse quickened. She watched the screens intently, her fingers hovering over the keyboard, ready to alert Dominic if anything went wrong. The tension was palpable, every second feeling like an eternity.

Finally, Matteo arrived, his demeanor cautious as he approached the warehouse. Sofia was already inside, coordinating the logistics. Vincent, as always, remained in the shadows, overseeing the operation with a keen eye.

Emily listened through the hidden microphones, picking up snippets of their conversation. Matteo was communicating with someone on a burner phone, giving updates about the shipment. Sofia was ensuring everything was in place, her voice steady but anxious. Vincent, true to form, was silent and observant, his presence intimidating.

When the rival family's men showed up to collect the fake shipment, Dominic's team moved in. They surrounded the warehouse, blocking all exits and cutting off any escape routes. Dominic himself entered the building, flanked by his most trusted enforcers.

Dominic's arrival caused a ripple of panic among the traitors. Matteo tried to bolt but was quickly subdued by Dominic's men. Sofia froze, her eyes wide with fear. Vincent, however, stood his ground, his expression unreadable.

"Well, well," Dominic said, his voice cold and commanding. "Look at what we have here."

Emily watched from her vantage point, her heart pounding as the scene unfolded. She felt a mix of satisfaction and apprehension, knowing this confrontation would determine the future of their uneasy alliance.

Matteo was dragged to the center of the warehouse, forced to his knees. Dominic approached him, his expression one of controlled fury.

"You thought you could betray me and get away with it?" Dominic asked, his voice low and dangerous.

Matteo stammered, trying to come up with an excuse, but Dominic cut him off. "Save it. I've heard enough."

* * *

He turned to Sofia, who was trembling. "And you, Sofia? I trusted you."

Tears welled in Sofia's eyes. "Dominic, I... I didn't mean to—"

"Enough," Dominic snapped. "I'll deal with you later."

Finally, he turned to Vincent. "I expected better from you, Vincent. You were my right hand."

Vincent's expression remained hard. "It was just business, Dominic. Nothing personal."

"Business?" Dominic's voice dripped with contempt. "You call selling out your family business?"

Dominic's anger was palpable, and for a moment, it seemed like he might lash out. But then he took a deep breath, reigning in his fury. He needed to stay focused, to think clearly.

"Take them away," he ordered his men. "We'll deal with them later."

As Matteo, Sofia, and Vincent were led away, Dominic turned and walked out of the warehouse, heading toward the building where Emily was stationed. She watched him approach, her heart racing with anticipation.

When he entered the room, their eyes met, and for a moment, neither of them spoke. The intensity of the moment was overwhelming, the air charged with unspoken emotions.

"You did well," Dominic said finally, his voice softening slightly.

Emily nodded, her throat tight. "So did you."

There was a moment of silence, the tension between them almost unbearable. Then, without warning, Dominic closed the distance between them, his eyes burning with intensity.

* * *

"You're something else, Emily," he said, his voice low and husky. "I've never met anyone like you."

Emily's breath caught in her throat. The attraction she had felt before was stronger now, undeniable. She knew it was dangerous, that getting involved with Dominic was a risk, but she couldn't help herself.

"You're not so bad yourself," she replied, her voice trembling slightly.

Dominic reached out, his hand cupping her cheek. "This is crazy," he murmured. "But I can't stop thinking about you."

Emily's heart pounded in her chest. "Dominic, we shouldn't—"

"I know," he interrupted, his thumb brushing lightly against her skin. "But I don't care."

Before she could protest, he leaned in and kissed her, the intensity of the moment washing over them both. It was a kiss filled with pent-up desire, a release of the tension that had been building between them.

When they finally pulled apart, both of them were breathless. Emily's mind was spinning, the reality of what had just happened sinking in.

"We need to focus," she said, trying to regain her composure. "We still have a lot of work to do."

Dominic nodded, though his eyes still burned with desire. "You're right. We need to finish this."

They spent the next few hours going over the details of the plan, ensuring that everything was in place to deal with the traitors and secure Dominic's operations. Despite the intense emotions between them, they managed to stay focused on the task at hand.

As dawn approached, Emily felt a sense of accomplishment. They had taken a significant step toward uncovering the truth and securing their positions. But she also knew that this was only the beginning. The road ahead would be dangerous, filled with risks and challenges.

* * *

Emily and Dominic's partnership was now firmly established, bound by mutual goals and an undeniable attraction. They knew that working together was their best chance of success, even if it meant navigating the dangerous waters of their complicated relationship.

As they parted ways that morning, there was a sense of understanding between them. They were in this together, for better or worse.

Emily returned to her apartment, exhausted but determined. She had made significant progress, but there was still so much to do. The traitors had been exposed, but the full extent of the conspiracy was yet to be uncovered.

Dominic, meanwhile, prepared to deal with the fallout within his organization. He knew that trust would be hard to rebuild, but with Emily by his side, he felt more confident than ever.

Their partnership was just beginning, and the stakes were higher than ever. But they were ready to face whatever came their way, together.

As Emily settled into bed, her mind racing with thoughts of the day's events, she couldn't help but feel a spark of hope. They were making progress, and with Dominic's protection, she felt a little safer.

But she also knew that this was just the start of their journey. There would be more challenges, more dangers, and more intense moments ahead.

And through it all, the tension between them would continue to simmer, a constant reminder of the complicated relationship they had forged.

Emily closed her eyes, a sense of determination settling over her. She was ready for whatever came next.

Chapter Seven

The next morning, Emily awoke with a mix of excitement and trepidation. She had agreed to work with Dominic, and now it was time to immerse herself in his world. As she prepared for the day, her mind raced with the possibilities and dangers that lay ahead. She needed to be at her best—sharp, focused, and ready for anything.

Dominic had arranged for her to meet him at one of his private training facilities. Located in a secluded part of the city, it was a place where his men honed their skills away from prying eyes. As Emily arrived, she was struck by the high-tech security measures and the sheer size of the complex. It was a stark reminder of the power and resources Dominic wielded.

She was greeted by one of Dominic's trusted lieutenants, a burly man named Luca. He led her through the facility, explaining the various training areas and equipment. Emily listened carefully, taking in every detail. She needed to understand this world if she was going to survive in it.

Finally, they reached a large, open training room. Dominic was there, dressed in athletic gear, his muscular frame exuding strength and confidence. He looked up as they entered, his gaze locking onto Emily's. She felt a flutter of nerves but pushed it aside, determined to show no weakness.

"Emily," Dominic greeted her with a nod. "Welcome to my world."

* * *

She gave a curt nod in return. "Let's get started."

Dominic led her to the center of the room, where mats were laid out for hand-to-hand combat training. "Before we begin, I need to know what you're capable of," he said. "Show me what you've got."

Emily squared her shoulders, taking a deep breath. She had trained in self-defense and martial arts as part of her PI work, but she knew Dominic's level of expertise would be far beyond anything she had encountered before. She assumed a defensive stance, ready for his attack.

Dominic moved with lightning speed, launching a series of strikes and kicks that tested her reflexes and agility. Emily blocked and countered as best she could, but it was clear that Dominic was holding back, assessing her abilities. Despite his restraint, she found herself struggling to keep up with his speed and strength.

After a few minutes, Dominic stepped back, a hint of a smile playing at the corners of his mouth. "Not bad," he said. "You've got good instincts. But you need to be faster and more precise."

He moved behind her, adjusting her stance and demonstrating proper techniques. His hands were firm and confident, guiding her movements with precision. Emily couldn't help but notice the electricity that sparked every time he touched her, the sexual tension between them growing with each close call and accidental brush of skin.

For the next few hours, Dominic put Emily through a rigorous training regimen. He taught her advanced self-defense techniques, focusing on speed, accuracy, and adaptability. They practiced grappling, striking, and evasion, each session pushing Emily to her limits.

Throughout their training, the playful banter and underlying attraction between them were impossible to ignore. Dominic challenged her constantly, his teasing remarks both infuriating and exhilarating.

"Come on, Emily," he taunted as she struggled to break free from a hold. "You can do better than that."

* * *

She shot him a glare, her determination only intensifying. "I'm just getting started."

Dominic laughed, the sound rich and full of amusement. "That's the spirit. Show me what you've got."

As the days went on, Emily's skills improved, and so did her confidence. She learned to anticipate Dominic's moves, using her agility and quick thinking to outmaneuver him. Their training sessions became a dance of sorts, a blend of combat and chemistry that left them both breathless and exhilarated.

Emily stood in the dimly lit training room, her muscles already aching from the previous drills. Dominic decided it was time to teach Emily knife defense. He handed her a training knife, its blunt edge safe for practice but still capable of inflicting a painful bruise. They faced off, the tension between them palpable.

"Remember, always keep your eye on the blade," Dominic instructed. "And never let your guard down." Dominic watched her with a critical eye, his stance unwavering. He wasn't just an instructor—he was a force of nature, every move calculated, every demand pushing her further.

Emily nodded, her focus intense. Dominic lunged at her, and she dodged, countering with a swift move that almost caught him off guard. He grinned, clearly pleased with her progress.

"Good," he said. "But you need to be faster."

"Again," he ordered, his deep voice sending a ripple down her spine.

Emily exhaled sharply, adjusting her grip on the training knife. Sweat trickled down her back, the heat of exertion mingling with the tension thickening the air between them. She lunged, aiming for his side, but Dominic sidestepped with ease, catching her wrist and twisting just enough to send her off balance. She hit the mat with a frustrated grunt.

Before she could get up, he was there, crouching beside her. His grip tightened around her wrist, his touch firm but not painful. "You hesitate when you're unsure. The moment you second-guess yourself, you've already lost."

Emily's jaw clenched as she yanked her hand free. "Or maybe you're just too good at this."

A smirk tugged at the corner of his lips. "Flattery won't get you out of training. Now, up."

She pushed herself up, determination burning in her eyes. This was more than training—it was a battle of wills. Dominic challenged her in ways no one else ever had. He didn't coddle or soften his words; he expected more from her, and somehow, she wanted to prove she could be more.

They went through the motions again—strike, block, counter. Each time, Dominic corrected her form, sometimes guiding her movements with a touch that sent an unexpected jolt through her. Her body was exhausted, but something deeper burned within her—a mixture of frustration, admiration, and something else she refused to name.

One evening, after hours of relentless sparring, Dominic knocked her off her feet again. This time, Emily didn't stay down. She rolled onto her back and kicked out, catching him off guard. He stumbled back a step, surprise flickering across his face before it was replaced with something else—something unreadable.

Breathing heavily, she scrambled up. "Didn't see that one coming, did you?"

Dominic wiped a bead of sweat from his brow, eyes dark with approval. "Good. That's what I need from you."

The air between them grew thick, the line between mentor and student blurring. His gaze lingered on her longer than it should have, but he turned away before she could decipher the look in his eyes.

The next day, the drills became more brutal. Dominic didn't let up, forcing Emily to react faster, move smarter. When she slipped, he was there to correct her, his touch lingering just a second too long. She told herself it was nothing, but the way her pulse quickened every time they clashed said otherwise.

By the third day, exhaustion crept into her limbs, but her will remained unshaken. She wouldn't let Dominic see weakness—not now. When he charged at her in a simulated attack, she dodged at the last second, countering with a strike that nearly grazed his ribs. His low chuckle sent a shiver through her.

"Finally," he murmured. "You're starting to fight like you mean it."

They continued sparring, the pace quickening with each exchange. Suddenly, Dominic's foot slipped on the mat, and he stumbled, reaching out to steady himself. His hand landed on Emily's waist, pulling her close to him.

For a moment, they were frozen, their faces inches apart. Emily could feel the heat radiating from his body, the intensity of his gaze searing into her. Her breath caught in her throat, and she wondered if he could hear the rapid pounding of her heart.

Dominic's grip tightened, his eyes darkening with desire. "Emily..." he murmured, his voice low and husky.

She swallowed hard, trying to regain her composure. "We... we should keep training," she stammered, though her body betrayed her, leaning into his touch.

Dominic's lips curved into a slow, knowing smile. "Right. Training."

He released her, the moment passing but leaving a lingering charge in the air. They resumed their practice, but the close call had heightened the tension between them to an almost unbearable level.

As the weeks went by, Emily and Dominic's training sessions became a crucial part of their daily routine. They spent hours together, honing her skills and building a bond of trust and mutual respect. Dominic pushed her harder than anyone ever had, and in return, Emily challenged him in ways he hadn't expected.

* * *

One evening, after an especially grueling session, they sat on the edge of the mat, catching their breath. Dominic handed her a bottle of water, their fingers brushing in the exchange.

"You're getting better," he said, his tone genuine. "You're tougher than you look."

Emily smiled, taking a sip of water. "I've had to be. This line of work isn't for the faint-hearted."

Dominic studied her for a moment, his expression thoughtful. "Why did you become a PI, Emily? What drives you?"

She hesitated, the question bringing back memories she usually kept buried. But something about Dominic made her want to open up, to share the part of herself she guarded so closely.

"I almost lost someone close to me," she said quietly. "My brother. He got caught up in something dangerous, and he never made it out. I became a PI to make sure that never happens to anyone else. To bring justice to those who can't find it on their own."

Dominic's eyes softened, a rare glimpse of vulnerability in his otherwise stoic demeanor. "I'm sorry, Emily. I know what it's like to lose someone."

She looked at him, surprised by the sincerity in his voice. "Who did you lose?"

He took a deep breath, his gaze distant. "My sister. She was killed in a power struggle within the family. It's why I do what I do. To protect the people I care about, to make sure her death wasn't in vain."

For a moment, they sat in silence, the weight of their shared losses creating a deeper connection between them. It was a bond forged in pain and strengthened by their determination to survive and protect those they cared about.

As their training continued, Emily found herself relying more on Dominic, not just as a mentor but as an ally. They worked together seamlessly, their partnership growing stronger with each passing day. Despite the danger and the constant threat of betrayal, she began to trust him in ways she hadn't thought possible.

Dominic, too, was changing. Emily's presence had a profound impact on him, challenging his beliefs and forcing him to confront the darker aspects of his world. He admired her strength and resilience, qualities that mirrored his own but were tempered by a sense of justice he had long abandoned.

Chapter Eight

By the end of their training, Emily was at her limit. Every muscle ached, every movement sent pain shooting through her body. But she refused to quit. She had something to prove— to Dominic, to herself.

That night, they trained alone. The others had long since gone, but Dominic remained, watching her with that same unyielding intensity. When she lunged at him, there was more than just determination behind the strike—there was fire.

Dominic caught her wrist mid-air, twisting her around until her back was pressed against his chest. His breath was warm against her ear. "You're holding back."

Emily's heart pounded. "I'm giving everything I have."

His grip tightened slightly. "No, you're not. You're afraid to let go. Afraid of what happens when you stop thinking and just feel."

Her breath hitched. The words cut deeper than she expected. She wasn't sure if they were still talking about training.

The silence stretched, thick and charged. Then, slowly, he released her. Emily turned to face him, her pulse racing. Whatever was happening between them, it was growing, shifting into something dangerous.

Dominic stepped back, voice measured. "Again."

* * *

Emily rolled her eyes and continued. She wouldn't let Dominic think she couldn't handle the training.

One evening, after a particularly intense sparring session, Dominic pulled her aside. "Emily, there's something I need to show you."

He led her to a hidden room within the training facility, a space filled with monitors and surveillance equipment. On the screens were live feeds of various locations around the city—warehouses, docks, and safe houses.

"This is my network," Dominic explained. "I use it to keep an eye on my operations, to stay ahead of my enemies."

Emily was impressed by the sophistication of his setup. "You're always watching," she murmured, understanding the level of control he maintained.

Dominic nodded. "It's how I stay in power. But it's also how I protect those who matter to me."

He turned to her, his expression serious. "You're part of this now, Emily. You need to know everything."

Emily felt a surge of gratitude and responsibility. She was no longer an outsider; she was part of something bigger, a partnership that could change both their lives.

One night, their training took a more personal turn. Dominic decided it was time for Emily to learn how to handle firearms, a skill essential for her survival in his world. They went to the shooting range, where Dominic handed her a sleek, black handgun.

"Have you ever fired a gun before?" he asked.

Emily shook her head. "No. I've always relied on other means of defense."

Dominic guided her through the basics, his hands steady as he demonstrated the proper grip and stance. "It's all about control," he said, his voice calm and reassuring. "Control your breathing, your movements. Become one with the weapon."

Emily followed his instructions, her hands shaking slightly as she aimed at the target. Dominic stood close behind her, his presence both comforting and distracting.

"Take a deep breath," he murmured, his breath warm against her ear. "Focus."

She did as he said, her finger squeezing the trigger. The gunshot echoed in the range, and Emily felt a rush of adrenaline as she saw the bullet hit the target, albeit slightly off-center.

"Not bad," Dominic said, his voice filled with pride. "You'll get the hang of it."

They continued practicing, and with each shot, Emily's confidence grew. Dominic's guidance was patient and thorough, his touch sending shivers down her spine every time he corrected her form.

After their session, they returned to the training room, both of them exhilarated and exhausted. The tension between them had reached a breaking point, the close calls and accidental touches finally taking their toll.

As they stood facing each other, the air between them crackling with electricity, Dominic took a step closer, his eyes locked on hers. "Emily," he whispered, his voice thick with emotion.

She felt her heart race, her breath catching in her throat. "Dominic…"

He reached out, his hand cupping her cheek, his touch sending a jolt of desire through her body. "I can't fight this anymore," he murmured, his lips inches from hers.

Before she could respond, he closed the distance, capturing her lips in a kiss that was both fierce and tender. Emily felt herself melt into his embrace, the world around them fading away as they gave in to the undeniable attraction that had been building for weeks.

* * *

Their kiss deepened, the intensity of their connection overwhelming them both. They clung to each other, their bodies pressed together, the heat between them almost unbearable.

When they finally pulled apart, both of them were breathless, their hearts pounding. Emily looked into Dominic's eyes, seeing a mixture of desire and something deeper, something she hadn't expected.

"Emily," he said softly, his voice filled with emotion. "I need you. Not just as an ally, but as something more."

She felt a surge of emotion, her heart swelling with a mixture of fear and hope. "Dominic, I… I don't know what this means."

He smiled, his expression tender. "We'll figure it out together. One step at a time."

As they stood there, holding each other, Emily knew that their partnership had changed. It was no longer just about survival and strategy; it was about something deeper, something that could reshape both their lives.

They had a long road ahead, filled with dangers and challenges, but for the first time, Emily felt a sense of hope. She wasn't alone anymore. She had Dominic by her side, and together, they could face whatever came their way.

As they left the training room, hand in hand, Emily couldn't help but feel that this was the beginning of something extraordinary. They were no longer just allies; they were partners in every sense of the word, bound by a shared purpose and an undeniable connection.

And whatever the future held, they would face it together. The days following Emily and Dominic's intense training sessions were filled with a flurry of activity. Dominic had received intel about a significant shipment of illegal weapons that one of his rivals was planning to move through the city. It was an opportunity to strike a major blow against his enemies, but it required precise execution and absolute trust in his team—especially in Emily.

* * *

They had spent the last 48 hours planning the operation, going over every detail to ensure nothing was left to chance. Emily's hacking skills had proven invaluable, allowing them to intercept communications and gain critical insights into the rival's plans. Now, as they prepared to put their plan into action, the tension in the air was palpable.

The operation was set to take place in an abandoned warehouse near the docks, a labyrinthine structure with multiple entry points and hidden passages. It was the perfect place for an ambush, but it also meant that any mistake could lead to disaster.

Emily and Dominic arrived at the warehouse just after midnight, dressed in black and armed with an array of weapons and gadgets.

Dominic's men were already in position, their eyes scanning the area for any signs of trouble. The air was thick with anticipation, every shadow and sound amplifying the sense of danger.

"Are you ready for this?" Dominic asked, his voice low and steady.

Emily nodded, her expression determined. "Let's do it."

The plan was simple: Dominic's men would create a diversion at the front of the warehouse while Emily and Dominic slipped inside through a hidden entrance at the back. From there, they would make their way to the control room, where Emily would hack into the security system and disable the cameras and alarms.

As they moved through the darkened corridors, the tension between them was almost tangible. Their footsteps were silent, their movements synchronized, a testament to the bond they had forged through their training. Every so often, their hands would brush against each other, sending jolts of electricity through their bodies.

Suddenly, they heard voices approaching. Dominic signaled for Emily to follow him into a narrow alcove, their bodies pressed tightly together to avoid detection. The space was so tight that they could feel each other's breath, their faces inches apart.

Emily's heart pounded in her chest, the proximity to Dominic making it hard to focus. She could feel the heat of his body, his scent intoxicatingly close. Her mind raced with a mixture of fear and desire, the intensity of the moment almost overwhelming.

"Stay quiet," Dominic whispered, his lips brushing against her ear. "They'll pass by in a minute."

Emily nodded, her breath hitching at the feel of his lips so close to her skin. She tried to steady her breathing, but the combination of adrenaline and attraction made it nearly impossible.

The voices grew louder, the sound of footsteps echoing through the corridor. Emily pressed herself closer to Dominic, her body instinctively seeking his protection. His arms wrapped around her, holding her securely, and for a moment, she forgot about the mission, lost in the sensation of his touch.

As the voices began to fade, Emily felt a surge of relief. But just as she started to relax, Dominic's hand moved to her chin, tilting her face up to meet his gaze. The intensity in his eyes took her breath away, and she knew, in that instant, that the tension between them was about to reach its breaking point.

"Emily," Dominic murmured, his voice rough with emotion. "I shouldn't want this, but I do. Tell me to stop."

Before she could respond, his lips were on hers, the kiss fierce and passionate. Emily's initial shock melted away, replaced by a flood of desire as she kissed him back, her arms wrapping around his neck. The world around them faded into the background, the only thing that mattered was the connection they shared.

Their kiss deepened, their bodies pressed even closer together. Emily felt the fire of his touch, the way his hands roamed over her back, pulling her tighter against him. She responded with equal fervor, her fingers threading through his hair, holding him to her as if he were her lifeline.

When they finally pulled apart, both were breathless, their hearts racing. For a moment, they simply stared at each other, the reality of what had just happened sinking in. The air between them was charged with a mixture of passion and uncertainty, the consequences of their actions looming over them.

"We should—" Emily started, her voice shaky.

"Focus on the mission," Dominic finished for her, though his eyes were still dark with desire. "We can't afford any distractions."

Emily nodded, though her mind was spinning. "Right. The mission."

They stepped out of the alcove, their professional masks slipping back into place. But the memory of the kiss lingered, a constant reminder of the unresolved tension between them.

They made their way to the control room without further incident. Emily quickly set to work, her fingers flying over the keyboard as she hacked into the security system. She could feel Dominic's eyes on her, his presence both reassuring and distracting.

"Got it," she said after a few minutes, her voice filled with triumph. "Cameras and alarms are disabled."

"Good work," Dominic replied, his tone professional. "Now let's move."

They navigated through the warehouse, their senses on high alert. The plan was to intercept the shipment and gather evidence of the rival family's illegal activities. It was a risky move, but one that could cripple their enemies if successful.

As they approached the storage area, they heard the sound of vehicles and voices. Dominic signaled for his men to move into position, preparing for the ambush. Emily felt a surge of adrenaline, her body tensing in anticipation.

The next few minutes were a blur of action. Dominic's men moved swiftly and silently, subduing the guards and securing the area. Emily stayed close to Dominic, her eyes scanning for any signs of danger. She could feel the weight of the moment, knowing that any mistake could be fatal.

When they reached the storage area, they found the shipment—crates of illegal weapons, carefully hidden among legitimate goods. Emily quickly set up her equipment, documenting the evidence while Dominic coordinated with his men.

"Emily, we need to move," Dominic said, his voice urgent. "They'll be here any minute."

Emily nodded, her focus unwavering. She finished securing the evidence and packed up her gear, ready to make their escape. But just as they were about to leave, they heard the sound of approaching footsteps—more guards, alerted to their presence.

"Damn it," Dominic muttered. "We need to go, now."

They raced through the corridors, their hearts pounding. The sound of pursuit grew louder, the tension escalating with each passing second. Emily could feel Dominic's hand on her arm, guiding her, protecting her. She knew they were in this together, their fates intertwined.

As they reached the exit, Dominic's men provided cover, holding off the guards long enough for Emily and Dominic to slip out. They ran through the darkened streets, the cold night air biting at their skin. Emily's lungs burned, her muscles screaming in protest, but she pushed herself to keep going.

Finally, they reached a safe house, a small, unassuming building hidden in a quiet part of the city. Dominic ushered her inside, slamming the door shut behind them. They leaned against the wall, trying to catch their breath, the adrenaline still coursing through their veins.

"We made it," Emily said, her voice filled with a mix of relief and disbelief.

Dominic nodded, his expression intense. "You did great."

For a moment, they simply looked at each other, the weight of the night's events settling over them. The memory of their kiss lingered, a reminder of the connection they shared. But there was no time to dwell on it; they had a mission to complete, and their enemies wouldn't rest.

They quickly got to work, analyzing the evidence and planning their next move. Emily's mind raced with thoughts of the kiss, the feel of Dominic's lips on hers, but she forced herself to focus. The stakes were too high to let emotions cloud her judgment.

As they went over the details, Dominic's demeanor was all business, but Emily could see the flicker of something more in his eyes. She knew he was struggling with the same feelings, the same attraction that had brought them to this point.

"We need to get this information to our contacts," Dominic said, his voice steady. "It's the key to taking down our enemies."

Emily nodded, her resolve firm. "I'll handle it."

As they prepared to leave the safe house, Emily felt a sense of determination. They had a mission to complete, and she was more committed than ever to seeing it through. But she also knew that the kiss had changed things between them, adding a new layer of complexity to their partnership.

"Emily," Dominic said, his voice softer now. "About earlier..."

She looked at him, her heart aching with a mixture of hope and fear. "Dominic, we can't afford to be distracted. We have to focus on the mission."

He nodded, though she could see the struggle in his eyes. "I know. But this isn't over. We'll deal with it, one step at a time."

Emily felt a surge of emotion, a mixture of relief and anticipation. She knew they had a long road ahead, filled with danger and uncertainty. But for now, they had a mission to complete, and that was their top priority.

As they stepped out into the night, ready to face whatever challenges lay ahead, Emily couldn't help but feel a sense of hope. They were partners, allies, and perhaps something more. And whatever the future held, they would face it together, one step at a time.

Chapter Nine

The opulent grandeur of the gathering was overwhelming. Emily adjusted the sleek black dress that clung to her curves, checking her reflection one last time in the gilded mirror. Her platinum blonde hair cascaded in soft waves, framing her face, while a hint of red lipstick accentuated her full lips. She looked every part the sophisticated socialite she was meant to be tonight.

Dominic had given her detailed instructions: a high-profile mafia gathering at an extravagant estate. It was a chance to gather vital intel on rival operations—a critical mission that required Emily's unique skill set. As she approached the entrance, her heart raced with both excitement and apprehension.

The estate was a sprawling palace, its grandeur accentuated by the sprawling gardens and majestic fountains. The evening air was crisp, the soft hum of classical music filtering through the open windows. Emily handed her invitation to the doorman, who gave her a courteous nod before ushering her inside. The opulence was staggering—crystal chandeliers hung from the ceiling, their light dancing on the polished marble floors. Guests mingled in lavish attire, their conversations a murmur of intrigue and power.

Emily scanned the crowd, her eyes sharp despite her relaxed demeanor. She had to blend in, gather information, and stay under the radar. The mission was risky, but she was determined to succeed. As she moved through the crowd, her gaze was drawn to a group of men huddled in a corner, their hushed tones suggesting a serious discussion. She recognized a few of them from Dominic's intel—key players in the rival's operations.

Emily made her way towards the bar, subtly keeping an eye on the group. She ordered a drink, her movements smooth and confident. Her mind was a whirl of strategy and precaution. If she could get close enough to overhear their conversation or spot any documents, it would be a major win.

As she sipped her drink, a towering figure approached—one of Luca's enforcers. He was imposing, with a scar running down his cheek that added to his menacing presence. Emily could feel his eyes on her, the weight of his scrutiny almost tangible. She forced a smile, her nerves on edge.

"New face around here?" he asked, his voice a low growl.

Emily maintained her composure. "Just passing through. I'm a friend of a friend."

The enforcer's gaze hardened, his suspicion clear. "You sure you're not here for other reasons?"

Before Emily could respond, a voice cut through the tension. "Is everything alright here?"

Dominic appeared, his demeanor commanding as always. He was impeccably dressed in a tailored suit, his presence immediately shifting the atmosphere. The enforcer's hostility melted away, replaced by a look of deference.

"No problem, boss," the enforcer muttered, retreating into the crowd.

Dominic's eyes locked with Emily's, a flicker of concern and frustration in their depths. "We need to talk," he said tersely.

Emily's heart sank. Dominic's presence was both a relief and a complication. She followed him through a side door, away from the bustling crowd.

* * *

Back at the safe house, the air was thick with tension. Dominic paced the room, his frustration evident. Emily stood by the window, her arms crossed, her mind racing with the details of the night.

"Do you have any idea how dangerous that was?" Dominic's voice was low but intense. "You could have been compromised, or worse."

Emily's jaw tightened. "I managed to get the information we need. Isn't that what matters?"

Dominic's eyes flared with anger. "It's not just about the information. It's about your safety. You went into a high-risk situation with no backup. What if something had happened?"

Emily's own frustration bubbled over. "I'm not helpless, Dominic. I've done this before. I can take care of myself."

Dominic's face was a mask of frustration and concern. "This isn't just another job. I care about you. I can't stand the thought of losing you."

His words were like a punch to the gut. Emily's anger faltered, replaced by a wave of emotion. She took a step closer, her eyes meeting his. "You're not the only one worried, Dominic. I'm doing this because it's important, not because I want to put myself in danger."

Dominic's expression softened, his gaze searching hers. "I know you're capable. But this is more than just a mission. It's personal for me."

Emily's heart pounded. The raw honesty in his voice was disarming. She had seen Dominic's tough exterior, but this moment revealed a vulnerability that was both unexpected and deeply affecting.

"Why does it matter so much?" Emily asked quietly.

Dominic's gaze never wavered. "Because I've lost people before. I can't bear the thought of losing you too."

The room was charged with an electric tension as the intensity of their emotions clashed. Emily could feel the weight of Dominic's words, the depth of his concern cutting through her own frustration. The mission had been dangerous, but Dominic's reaction was more personal than she had anticipated.

Before either of them could say more, Dominic's hand reached out, his fingers brushing against Emily's cheek. The touch was gentle, a stark contrast to the heated argument that had preceded it. Emily's breath caught in her throat as Dominic's eyes searched hers with a mixture of longing and vulnerability.

"I don't want to fight with you," Dominic said softly. "I just want you to be safe."

Emily's heart ached at the sincerity in his voice. She reached up, her hand covering his. "I'm sorry. I didn't mean to upset you. I just... I needed to get the intel. It was important."

Dominic's thumb gently brushed her cheek. "I understand. But please, promise me you'll be more careful."

Emily nodded, her throat tight. "I promise."

Dominic pulled her into a fierce hug, his arms wrapping around her tightly. Emily clung to him, her own emotions swirling in a tumultuous mix of relief and affection. The argument had stripped away the pretense, revealing the raw, unfiltered connection they shared.

As they pulled apart, their faces close, the tension between them was palpable. The argument had forged a deeper bond, one built on mutual understanding and genuine care. The night had been fraught with danger, but it had also brought them closer in ways neither of them had fully anticipated.

Emily took a deep breath, her mind racing with the implications of their shared experience. The mission had been successful, but the emotional fallout was just beginning. She knew that whatever challenges lay ahead, they would face them together—stronger and more connected than ever before.

Dominic's eyes softened as he looked at her, a mixture of relief and affection in his gaze. "We'll get through this. Together."

Emily nodded, a small smile touching her lips. "Together."

As they stood there in the quiet of the safe house, the weight of the night's events settled over them. The mission had tested their resolve, but it had also deepened their connection. They were no longer just partners in a dangerous game—they were allies bound by something far more profound.

And as they faced the uncertain future, Emily felt a renewed sense of hope. They had weathered the storm together, and whatever lay ahead, they would face it as one.

Chapter Ten

The safe house was tense with anticipation. Dominic had spent the last few weeks meticulously tracking every piece of information Emily had gathered about the suspected traitor within his organization. The revelation had come in a series of encrypted messages, painstakingly decoded by Emily's skilled hands. The traitor, it seemed, was none other than Marco, one of Dominic's most trusted lieutenants.

The weight of the betrayal was heavy. Marco had been a key player in Dominic's operations, his loyalty unquestioned—until now. The sense of betrayal cut deep, especially for Dominic, who had always prided himself on loyalty and trust within his ranks.

Dominic's office was dimly lit, the atmosphere charged with a grim seriousness. Emily sat across from Dominic, the flickering light from the desk lamp casting shadows across her face. Dominic's expression was a mixture of anger and resolve, his gaze fixed on the file containing the evidence of Marco's treachery.

"Are you sure about this?" Dominic's voice was low, his tone edged with frustration.

Emily nodded, her gaze steady. "The evidence is clear. Marco's been feeding information to Luca's people. We need to confront him and deal with this before it spirals further."

Dominic's jaw tightened. "I never thought Marco would turn against me. He's been with me through everything."

* * *

Emily reached out, her hand briefly touching Dominic's. "It's not your fault. Sometimes, betrayal comes from the places we least expect."

Dominic's eyes softened for a moment, his anger tempered by the realization of the gravity of the situation. "I need to handle this personally. Marco's betrayal has put everything at risk."

Emily nodded, her expression resolute. "I'll back you up. We need to make sure this is resolved without further bloodshed."

The confrontation was set to take place in an abandoned warehouse, a stark, empty space that had once served as a storage facility but now lay desolate and echoing with the sounds of the city outside. Dominic and Emily arrived separately, Dominic's black SUV pulling up first. He moved with a calculated, purposeful stride, his demeanor cold and focused. Emily followed shortly, her own nerves steeled for what lay ahead.

Inside the warehouse, the shadows loomed large, the sparse light from a single overhead bulb casting eerie shapes across the concrete floor. Dominic stood in the center of the space, his eyes scanning the surroundings with a predatory focus. Emily positioned herself strategically, her senses on high alert.

Marco emerged from the shadows, his face a mask of defiance and fear. He wore a leather jacket, his eyes darting nervously between Dominic and Emily.

"I know why you're here," Marco said, his voice trembling slightly. "You've figured it out."

Dominic's eyes were hard, his anger barely contained. "You've betrayed me, Marco. You've put everything at risk."

Marco's face twisted with a mix of guilt and desperation. "I had no choice. They threatened my family. I was trying to protect them."

Emily watched as Dominic's expression shifted from anger to a more somber understanding. "You should have come to me. We could have found a way."

Marco's eyes were pleading. "It was too late. They were watching my every move. I'm sorry, Dominic."

The tension in the room reached a breaking point. Dominic's hand moved to his side, where a concealed weapon was hidden. Marco, sensing the imminent danger, lunged for a nearby crate, pulling out a knife.

The warehouse erupted into chaos. Dominic and Marco clashed violently, their struggle intense and raw. Emily's heart raced as she moved to the sidelines, her mind racing with thoughts of how to intervene if necessary. The two men grappled fiercely, Marco's desperation evident in every swing of the knife.

Dominic fought with a controlled fury, his movements precise and calculated. Despite his anger, he seemed determined to avoid unnecessary harm. The struggle reached its climax as Dominic managed to disarm Marco, sending the knife skittering across the floor.

Marco fell to his knees, his face a mask of defeat and despair.

Dominic stood over him, breathing heavily, his eyes filled with a mixture of anger and sadness. "You're done, Marco. We'll deal with this later."

As Dominic turned to address Emily, a sharp pain registered on his face. He glanced down to see a deep gash on his side, blood seeping through his shirt. The sight of his injury sent a jolt of fear through Emily.

"Dominic!" she called out, rushing to his side. "You're hurt. We need to get you patched up."

Dominic's face was pale, the exertion of the fight taking its toll. He stumbled slightly, his strength waning. "It's nothing," he said through gritted teeth. "We need to get out of here."

Emily guided him toward the exit, her concern for his well-being overriding her anxiety. "We'll take care of this back at the safe house.

Just stay with me."

With Dominic's arm draped over her shoulder, they made their way to the safe house. Emily's mind raced as she worked to keep him focused and conscious. The drive was tense, the gravity of the situation weighing heavily on both of them.

Back at the safe house, Emily's hands were steady but her heart was in turmoil. She helped Dominic into a chair, her gaze fixed on the wound that needed immediate attention. The safe house, normally a refuge from the chaos, now felt like a sterile operating room.

"Let me see," Emily said, her voice firm but gentle. She carefully peeled back Dominic's shirt, her eyes widening at the extent of the injury. The gash was deep, and the blood flow was steady but manageable.

Dominic winced as Emily cleaned the wound, her touch careful and precise. She worked quickly, her movements practiced despite the urgency of the situation. She cleaned the wound thoroughly, her heart pounding with each movement.

"How bad is it?" Dominic asked, his voice strained.

Emily's gaze remained focused on her task. "It's deep, but it's not life-threatening. I need to stitch it up, though."

Dominic nodded, his face a mixture of pain and determination. "Do what you need to do."

As she prepared the stitching supplies, Emily could feel the weight of the situation pressing down on her. Dominic's vulnerability, coupled with the intensity of their earlier confrontation, had created a charged atmosphere. The room was filled with the faint smell of antiseptic and the sound of Dominic's labored breathing.

Emily's hands were steady as she worked, her concentration unbroken. She could feel Dominic's gaze on her, the intensity of his eyes reflecting a depth of emotion that was both reassuring and disconcerting. The process was meticulous, each stitch a testament to Emily's skill and care.

As she worked, Dominic's hand reached out, his fingers brushing against hers. The contact was electric, a reminder of the connection that had deepened between them. Emily looked up, meeting his gaze with a mixture of concern and affection.

"Thank you," Dominic said softly. "For everything."

Emily's heart ached at the sincerity in his voice. "You don't have to thank me. We're in this together."

The act of tending to Dominic's wounds had created a moment of intimacy that went beyond physical care. As Emily finished stitching and bandaged the wound, the silence in the room was filled with unspoken understanding. The danger they had faced, the violence they had endured, and the betrayal they had uncovered had all contributed to a deepening bond.

Dominic's eyes were soft as he looked at Emily, his gratitude evident. "I don't know what I'd do without you."

Emily's own emotions were on the edge of breaking through. The vulnerability she had seen in Dominic, coupled with the danger they had faced together, had forged a connection that was both profound and transformative. "I'm here for you, Dominic. No matter what."

Dominic's hand reached up to cup Emily's face, his touch tender and reassuring. "You mean more to me than you know. This night... it's shown me how much I need you."

Emily felt a lump in her throat, her emotions overwhelming. "I feel the same way. We've been through so much together, and it's only made us stronger."

They sat there in the quiet of the safe house, their closeness a balm for the emotional and physical wounds they had endured. Dominic's injury had been a stark reminder of the dangers they faced, but it had also brought them closer in a way neither of them had fully anticipated.

* * *

As the night wore on, Emily and Dominic shared their thoughts and fears, their conversations filled with a newfound depth of intimacy. They spoke of their pasts, their hopes for the future, and the challenges they faced. The connection between them was unspoken yet palpable, a bond forged in the crucible of danger and trust.

And as they lay together, the weight of the night's events settling over them, Emily knew that whatever lay ahead, they would face it together. Their bond was unbreakable, strengthened by their shared experiences and the deepening of their emotional connection.

Dominic's injury had been a catalyst for change, a moment that had revealed the true depth of their feelings for each other. As they faced the uncertain future, Emily felt a sense of hope and determination. They had survived the night's trials, and their connection was stronger than ever.

In the quiet of the safe house, with Dominic's hand in hers and the world outside fading away, Emily knew that they were ready to face whatever challenges lay ahead. Together, they would navigate the complexities of their world and their relationship, their bond unbreakable and their commitment unwavering.

Chapter Eleven

The safe house, once a sanctuary of protection, had become a space of intense emotional and physical proximity. The events of the past few weeks had left Emily and Dominic both physically and emotionally exhausted. Dominic's injury, though healing, had served as a catalyst, bringing their emotional barriers to the forefront. The violence, betrayal, and danger had forged a connection between them that was undeniable.

That evening, the atmosphere was thick with a different kind of tension. The events of the day had left them both on edge, their proximity charged with unspoken desires. They had shared an intense experience of danger and vulnerability, which had created a profound sense of closeness between them.

Dominic was sprawled on the couch, his injured side carefully bandaged, but his demeanor was relaxed. Emily moved around the room with a quiet grace, her thoughts a tumultuous mix of concern and attraction. They had been dancing around their feelings for each other for weeks, their emotional and physical connection intensifying with each passing day.

The dim light from the lamps cast a warm glow around the room, creating an intimate setting that seemed to heighten their awareness of each other. Emily could feel the electricity in the air, a palpable reminder of the connection that had grown between them.

Dominic looked up from his seat, his eyes meeting Emily's with an intensity that made her heart race. "Emily," he said softly, his voice tinged with a raw vulnerability that struck a chord deep within her.

Emily paused, her gaze locked with his. "Dominic, what's on your mind?"

Dominic shifted on the couch, wincing slightly as he adjusted his position. "Tonight has been… overwhelming. Everything we've been through. I can't stop thinking about how close we've become."

Emily's breath caught in her throat. The intensity of Dominic's gaze, combined with the quiet of the room, made the moment feel charged with possibility. She moved closer, her heart pounding as she reached out to touch his shoulder.

"I feel it too," she admitted, her voice barely above a whisper. "We've been through so much, and it's only made me realize how much I care about you."

Dominic's hand covered hers, his touch warm and reassuring. "I've been trying to ignore it, to keep my distance. But I can't anymore. I need to be close to you."

The sincerity in his voice melted away any remaining reservations Emily had. She leaned in, her lips brushing against his in a tentative, exploratory kiss. The contact was electric, sending a shiver through both of them. Dominic's hands moved to cradle her face, his kiss deepening with a fervor that matched Emily's own growing desire.

The kiss quickly escalated into something more intense. Dominic's hands roamed over Emily's body, his touch igniting a fire within her. Emily responded with equal passion, her hands sliding up his chest, feeling the firm muscle beneath his shirt. The heat between them was overwhelming, a physical manifestation of the emotional connection they shared.

Dominic's hands moved to the hem of Emily's dress, his fingers brushing against her skin as he lifted it slowly. The sensation of his touch against her bare skin sent waves of pleasure through her. Emily's breath came in quick gasps as she guided Dominic's hands to the fastenings of her dress, her fingers deftly working to free it.

As the dress fell to the floor, Dominic's eyes were filled with a mixture of admiration and desire. He took in the sight of Emily, her body illuminated by the soft light of the room. The vulnerability and trust they had built over the weeks were now being expressed in the most intimate way possible.

Dominic's hands explored her body with a reverent touch, his lips trailing kisses along her neck and shoulders. Emily's body responded instinctively, her hands gripping his shoulders as she pressed closer to him. The intensity of their connection was undeniable, each touch and kiss deepening their bond.

The passion between them was overwhelming. Dominic lifted Emily effortlessly, carrying her to the bedroom. The space was dimly lit, the shadows creating an atmosphere of intimacy and anticipation. He placed her gently on the bed, his eyes never leaving hers as he continued to kiss her with a fervor that left her breathless.

As their bodies came together, the world outside seemed to disappear. The intensity of their desire was matched by the depth of their emotional connection. They moved together in a rhythm that was both primal and tender, their breaths mingling as they explored each other with a mixture of urgency and tenderness.

The heat of their lovemaking was all-consuming, a physical expression of the bond they had forged. Each touch, each kiss was an affirmation of their connection, a testament to the depth of their feelings for each other. The experience was mind-blowing, a culmination of the passion and desire that had been building between them.

The room was filled with the sounds of their pleasure, the intensity of their lovemaking leaving them both breathless and exhilarated. The physical connection they shared was profound, a reflection of the emotional depth that had been established between them.

As the waves of passion subsided, Emily and Dominic lay together, their bodies entwined and their breaths coming in slow, measured patterns. The room was quiet, the only sounds the soft rustle of the sheets and the occasional sigh. They lay there in a comfortable silence, the weight of the night's events settling over them.

Emily could feel the emotional intensity of the moment, a deep sense of vulnerability and connection that went beyond the physical. She turned to Dominic, her eyes searching his face for the reassurance that she needed.

Dominic looked at her with a mixture of affection and tenderness. "Emily, I've never felt this close to anyone before."

Emily's heart swelled at his words. She reached out to trace his jawline with her fingers, her touch gentle and reassuring. "I feel the same way. We've been through so much together, and it's only made us stronger."

Dominic's eyes were soft, filled with a depth of emotion that spoke volumes. "Tonight... it's changed everything. I know we're facing a lot of challenges, but I feel like we can get through anything as long as we're together."

Emily nodded, her own emotions mirrored in Dominic's gaze. "We've built something incredible together. I believe in us."

They lay there, wrapped in each other's arms, sharing their thoughts and fears. The intimacy they had shared had deepened their connection, creating a bond that went beyond physical attraction. They spoke of their pasts, their hopes for the future, and the challenges they faced. The conversation was filled with a raw honesty that revealed the depth of their feelings for each other.

Dominic spoke of his past—the loss of loved ones, the struggles of leading a mafia family, and the constant danger that surrounded him. Emily listened with empathy, her heart aching at the pain and challenges he had faced. She shared her own experiences—the loss of her parents, her decision to become a private investigator, and the drive that had fueled her quest for justice.

As they talked, the vulnerability they had shown during their lovemaking was mirrored in their conversation. They opened up to each other in ways they had never done before, their shared experiences creating a deeper understanding of one another.

Dominic's hand rested gently on Emily's, his touch a comforting presence. "I never imagined I'd find someone like you. You've brought so much light into my life, even in the midst of all this darkness."

Emily's eyes were filled with emotion as she looked at him. "You've given me a sense of belonging, a purpose. I've never felt so connected to someone before."

The intimacy they had shared had created a bond that was both profound and transformative. They lay together, their bodies close, the warmth of their connection a reassuring presence amid the uncertainty they faced.

As the night wore on, they continued to talk, their conversation flowing freely as they explored the depths of their feelings for each other. The connection they had forged was a testament to the strength of their bond, a reflection of the love and trust that had developed between them.

And as they drifted off to sleep, wrapped in each other's arms, Emily knew that their relationship had reached a new level of depth and intimacy. The challenges they had faced together had only strengthened their connection, and whatever lay ahead, they would face it together—stronger and more united than ever before.

In the quiet of the night, with Dominic's heartbeat steady against her own, Emily felt a profound sense of peace and contentment. Their love was a beacon of hope in the midst of the chaos, a reminder that they could face any challenge as long as they were together.

Chapter Twelve

The quiet hum of the safe house's air conditioner was a stark contrast to the chaos brewing outside. Dominic had tried to enjoy a rare moment of normalcy with Emily, but the undercurrent of tension was palpable. Their intimacy had brought them closer, but it had also made them vulnerable to the dangers lurking in the shadows.

Dominic had been working tirelessly to stabilize his position within the mafia and eliminate the remaining threats to his organization. The revelation of Marco's betrayal had stirred up not only internal dissent but also increased hostility from rival factions. The stability Dominic had fought so hard to maintain was now in jeopardy.

Emily, though aware of the risks, had chosen to remain by Dominic's side. Her decision had only solidified their bond but also made her a prime target for those who wished to exploit Dominic's vulnerabilities. The connection between them, once a source of solace, had become a strategic liability in the cutthroat world of organized crime.

The first signs of trouble came with an ominous phone call. Dominic was in his office, going over security reports, when his phone rang. The number was unfamiliar, but he answered it out of habit. The voice on the other end was cold and mocking, dripping with malicious intent.

"Dominic, I hope you're enjoying your little romance. We've decided to make things interesting."

* * *

The voice was unmistakable. It belonged to Luca Marino, a ruthless rival who had long coveted Dominic's position. Luca's tone was filled with a menacing satisfaction, making it clear that he was about to deliver devastating news.

"What do you want, Luca?" Dominic's voice was steady, though his heart pounded in his chest.

"Simple," Luca replied. "I want you to understand the cost of crossing me. We've taken someone important to you. Emily Williams is now our guest."

The words hit Dominic like a sledgehammer. Emily's name, so casually thrown into the conversation, sent a chill through him. "What have you done with her?"

"She's safe for now," Luca said, his voice dripping with insincerity. "But unless you want her to suffer, you'll make certain choices. There's a meeting place. Bring the evidence of your compliance, or she'll pay the price."

The call ended abruptly, leaving Dominic seething with rage and fear. The threat against

Emily was personal and direct. Dominic knew he couldn't afford to waste time. He had to act quickly to ensure her safety and deal with the treacherous situation that had unfolded.

Dominic's mind raced as he formulated a plan. His initial impulse was to go in guns blazing, but he knew that such an approach could endanger Emily's life further. He had to be strategic, balancing his emotions with the harsh realities of mafia politics.

He immediately called his most trusted operatives, gathering them in the war room. The room was dimly lit, the walls covered with maps and intelligence reports. Dominic's face was a mask of determination as he outlined his plan.

"Luca Marino has taken Emily," Dominic began, his voice steady despite the storm brewing inside him. "We need to rescue her without giving him the leverage he's seeking. We'll set up a trap and use his own tactics against him."

* * *

One of his operatives, Marco, now under tight scrutiny after his betrayal, shifted nervously. "We can't underestimate Luca. He's likely to have multiple layers of security and contingencies."

Dominic's gaze was unwavering. "We'll use that to our advantage. We'll create a diversion, draw his forces away from the real objective. Our priority is to get Emily out safely."

As the operatives dispersed to execute their respective roles, Dominic's thoughts were a whirlpool of anxiety and strategy. He knew that the upcoming operation required not only tactical precision but also emotional control. The safety of the woman he loved was on the line, and failure was not an option.

The rendezvous point was an abandoned warehouse on the outskirts of the city. It was a stark and ominous location, far from the prying eyes of law enforcement or any potential allies.

Dominic and his team arrived in the dead of night, their movements shrouded in secrecy.

The warehouse was a cavernous structure, its interior dark and filled with echoing footsteps. Dominic and his team entered through a side door, their approach silent and methodical. They had rigged the area with surveillance equipment and set up hidden positions to monitor the surroundings.

Dominic's eyes scanned the area, his heart racing with a mix of anticipation and dread. He could see shadows moving in the distance, the signs of Luca's men setting up their own defenses. The scene was set for a high-stakes confrontation.

After what felt like an eternity of waiting, Luca and his men arrived. Luca strode in with an air of arrogant confidence, his eyes scanning the area as if he owned it. He was flanked by several heavily armed guards, each of them a potential threat to Dominic's plan.

Dominic's jaw clenched as he saw Emily being pushed forward, her hands bound and a look of defiant determination on her face. Despite her predicament, she maintained her composure, a testament to her strength and resilience. The sight of her was both a relief and a source of renewed urgency.

"Good to see you've come prepared," Luca called out, his voice dripping with mockery. "Let's see if you've got what it takes to save your precious Emily."

Dominic stepped forward, his face a mask of controlled anger. "Release her, Luca. You don't want to make this any more complicated."

Luca's eyes gleamed with malicious satisfaction. "Ah, but I think I do. You see, Dominic, this is more than just a simple exchange. It's a test of your resolve. If you want her back, you'll have to prove it. And I assure you, I'm not making this easy."

As Luca spoke, Dominic's mind was racing, devising a plan to outwit his rival. He knew that rushing in would only play into Luca's hands. He needed to stay calm and use his resources effectively.

Luca gestured to one of his men, who stepped forward holding a briefcase. "Here's the evidence," Luca said. "Open it, and let's see what you've got."

Dominic nodded to one of his operatives, who moved to retrieve the briefcase from Luca's man. Inside, Dominic found the documents he needed, a mixture of fake and real information designed to mislead and manipulate. He examined them quickly, his mind racing to determine what was genuine and what was a trap.

The diversionary tactics had been set in motion. Dominic's team began to create disturbances around the perimeter, drawing some of Luca's men away from the central area. The noise and chaos were designed to disrupt Luca's operations and provide a window for Dominic to make his move.

In the midst of the confusion, Dominic's operatives stealthily moved into position, their goal clear: rescue Emily and neutralize the immediate threat posed by Luca's men. Dominic's heart pounded as he watched the scene unfold, his focus unwavering.

Luca's guards began to shift their attention toward the disturbances, creating an opening. Dominic seized the opportunity, signaling his team to move. The operation was fluid and precise, each member of the team executing their role with practiced efficiency.

As the team advanced, Dominic moved toward Emily, his heart in his throat. He could see the fear and determination in her eyes as he approached. Despite her precarious situation, she held her head high, a testament to her strength and resolve.

"Emily, we're getting you out of here," Dominic said, his voice filled with urgency.

Emily's eyes softened as she looked at Dominic. "Be careful. Luca won't make this easy."

Dominic nodded, his eyes scanning the area for any signs of imminent danger. The sounds of the ongoing chaos outside were a constant reminder of the precariousness of their situation. He worked quickly to free Emily from her restraints, his hands shaking slightly with the weight of the moment.

As Emily's bonds fell away, Dominic pulled her into a protective embrace. "We need to move. Now."

The team's efforts were paying off. The diversions had successfully drawn many of Luca's men away, but there were still threats to navigate. Dominic and Emily, along with the rest of the team, made their way through the warehouse, their movements swift and coordinated.

The tension was palpable as they neared the exit. The warehouse was a maze of shadows and obstacles, each turn and corner potentially hiding a threat. Dominic's focus was laser-sharp, his attention divided between ensuring Emily's safety and managing the ongoing conflict.

Just as they were about to reach the exit, Luca's remaining guards closed in. The confrontation was swift and intense, a flurry of gunfire and tactical maneuvers. Dominic's team engaged the guards with practiced precision, their training and experience evident in the efficiency of their response.

* * *

With the immediate threat neutralized, Dominic and Emily finally emerged from the warehouse, the cool night air a welcome relief from the oppressive atmosphere inside. The safe house was a short distance away, and they made their way there quickly, their focus on ensuring Emily's safety.

Once inside, Dominic wasted no time in checking Emily for any injuries. Despite her ordeal, she appeared to be physically unharmed, though the emotional toll was evident. Dominic's heart ached as he saw the exhaustion and fear in her eyes.

"Are you alright?" Dominic asked, his voice filled with concern.

Emily nodded, though her expression was tired. "I'm fine, just shaken. What about you? Did you get everything sorted with Luca?"

Dominic sighed, his frustration evident. "Luca's still out there. This isn't over. But we've managed to get you out safely, and that's what matters right now."

Emily reached out and took Dominic's hand, her touch a calming presence. "We'll handle it. Together."

As they settled into the safe house, the reality of the night's events began to sink in. The emotional and physical toll of the rescue was significant, but the bond between them had only deepened. The experience had solidified their connection, reinforcing the strength of their relationship.

Dominic took a moment to reflect on the events that had transpired. The danger, the confrontation, and the rescue had tested him in ways he hadn't anticipated. The vulnerability he felt in the face of Emily's abduction had been a stark reminder of how deeply he cared for her.

Emily, too, was processing the night's events. The fear and anxiety of the kidnapping had been overwhelming, but the support and determination of Dominic and his team had been a source of strength.
The bond they shared had proven resilient in the face of adversity.

* * *

As the night wore on, Dominic and Emily sat together, their conversation reflecting the depth of their emotions and the challenges they had faced. The ordeal had been a crucible for their relationship, testing their commitment and resolve.

"We've come through this stronger," Emily said, her voice filled with conviction. "Whatever happens next, we'll face it together."

Dominic nodded, his eyes filled with gratitude and affection. "We've proven that we can handle anything, as long as we're together. I won't let anything come between us."

The bond between them had been forged in the fires of conflict and danger, a testament to their strength and resilience. The night's events had only deepened their connection, creating a foundation of trust and commitment that would guide them through the challenges ahead.

As they embraced, the warmth of their connection provided a reassuring sense of stability. The future was uncertain, but their love and dedication to each other were unwavering. The experiences they had shared had strengthened their relationship, and they were ready to face whatever came next, united and resolute.

Chapter Thirteen

The air in the command center was heavy with tension. Dominic paced the room, his mind focused on the upcoming rescue mission. The warehouse raid had been a hard-fought victory, but it was only a preliminary step in a larger confrontation. Luca Marino's stronghold, a heavily fortified estate on the outskirts of the city, was the next target.

Dominic's team, composed of highly trained operatives, was prepped and ready. They were outfitted in tactical gear, their faces hidden behind masks and their weapons loaded and primed. The dim light of the command center flickered as Dominic reviewed the final details of the operation.

Emily had been a crucial part of the planning. Despite her recent ordeal, she had insisted on being involved. Her skills and intelligence were invaluable, but Dominic was determined to keep her out of direct danger. The previous kidnapping had been a stark reminder of how vulnerable she was in this high-stakes world.

"Are you sure about this?" Dominic asked Emily, his voice low but filled with concern. "We can keep you in a secure location while we handle this."

Emily's gaze was resolute, her expression a mix of determination and defiance. "I'm not sitting this one out. I've seen what they're capable of, and I want to be there to help. Besides, you're not going in alone."

Dominic hesitated, the worry in his eyes betraying his conflicted emotions. He knew better than to argue with her, especially given her recent display of courage and resilience. "Alright, but stay close and be careful."

Emily nodded, her resolve unwavering. The mission was a complex operation, and the stakes were higher than ever. Luca Marino's estate was a fortress, fortified with armed guards and surveillance systems. The plan was to breach the estate, locate the hostages, and neutralize any threats while minimizing casualties.

The team's approach was methodical and precise. They arrived at the perimeter of Luca's estate under the cover of darkness. The estate was an imposing structure, surrounded by high fences and guarded by a battalion of armed men. The moonlight cast eerie shadows on the walls, adding to the sense of foreboding.

Dominic and his team moved in silence, their footsteps barely audible against the ground. They used specialized equipment to disable the estate's surveillance systems, allowing them to approach undetected. The plan was to strike swiftly and decisively, taking advantage of the element of surprise.

As they reached the main gate, Dominic signaled for the team to take their positions. The gate was reinforced and electronically controlled, but Dominic's team had come prepared. One of the operatives, a tech specialist, set to work on bypassing the security system.

The gate creaked open slowly, revealing the sprawling grounds of the estate. Dominic and his team slipped through the opening, their movements coordinated and precise. They made their way toward the main building, navigating through the shadows and avoiding patrols.

Inside the estate, the atmosphere was tense. Luca's men were on high alert, their movements predictable but still a threat. Dominic's team worked with practiced efficiency, neutralizing guards and securing key areas of the estate.

Emily, despite her earlier insistence, remained close to Dominic. She had proven her capability during their previous encounters, and her presence was a source of both strength and reassurance. Her sharp eyes and quick reflexes were invaluable as they moved through the estate.

The interior of the estate was as imposing as its exterior. The grand hall was adorned with opulent furnishings, a stark contrast to the violence and danger that lurked within. Dominic's team advanced cautiously, their eyes scanning every corner for potential threats.

The mission's objective was clear: locate the hostages, including any remaining captives from the previous incidents, and extract them safely. Luca's stronghold was a labyrinth of corridors and rooms, each one potentially hiding danger.

Dominic led the team through the building, their progress slow but steady. They encountered resistance as they moved deeper into the estate. Luca's men were well-trained and prepared, but Dominic's team was equally skilled, their coordination and expertise evident in every move.

Emily played a crucial role in the operation, providing valuable intelligence and support. Her knowledge of the estate's layout and her keen observations helped guide the team through the maze of rooms and corridors.

As they approached the central control room, the intensity of the mission escalated. The control room was the nerve center of the estate, where Luca's operations were coordinated. It was heavily guarded, and Dominic knew that breaching it would be a significant challenge.

The team positioned themselves strategically, preparing for the inevitable confrontation.

Dominic's heart raced as he reviewed the plan once more, the weight of the operation pressing heavily on him. The success of the mission depended on their ability to maintain control and overcome the obstacles that lay ahead.

The control room was a chaotic scene. Luca and his remaining guards were on high alert, their movements frantic as they tried to manage the escalating situation. Dominic and his team entered the room with precision, their weapons ready and their tactics well-rehearsed.

* * *

The initial confrontation was swift and intense. Dominic's team engaged Luca's guards with practiced efficiency, their movements a blur of action and coordination. The room was filled with the sounds of gunfire and the clash of combat, each moment a testament to the high stakes of the mission.

Emily, despite the danger, fought with a determination that matched Dominic's own. Her skills in combat and her quick thinking were evident as she engaged enemies and provided crucial support to the team. Her presence in the midst of the chaos was both a source of strength and a reminder of the stakes involved.

The battle raged on, the control room becoming a battleground of wills and skill. Dominic's team fought with a combination of precision and intensity, their goal clear: neutralize the immediate threats and secure the area.

As the fight reached its climax, Dominic's focus was unwavering. He fought alongside his team, his movements a testament to his training and experience. His eyes never left Luca, who was positioned at the center of the chaos, orchestrating the defense of his stronghold.

In the midst of the confrontation, Emily found herself face-to-face with one of Luca's top enforcers. The enforcer was a formidable opponent, his size and strength a significant challenge. Despite the odds, Emily's resolve was unshaken.

She engaged the enforcer with a combination of agility and precision. Her training and experience were evident in every move, her attacks calculated and effective. The fight was intense, the clash of combat a testament to Emily's skill and determination.

As the battle raged around them, Dominic caught sight of Emily's struggle. His heart pounded with a mix of concern and admiration as he watched her fight. He knew that she was capable, but seeing her in action was a reminder of her strength and resilience.

The enforcer's attacks were powerful, but Emily's quick reflexes allowed her to evade and counter with precision. She fought with a combination of skill and courage, her movements fluid and controlled.

The struggle was intense, but Emily's determination was unwavering.

In a decisive move, Emily managed to disarm the enforcer, her strength and agility overcoming his initial advantage. The enforcer staggered back, his control of the situation slipping away. Emily took the opportunity to subdue him, her actions a testament to her badass side.

With the control room secured and the immediate threats neutralized, Dominic's team turned their attention to the next phase of the operation: the rescue and escape. The estate was still a dangerous place, and they needed to extract the hostages and get out before reinforcements arrived.

Dominic and Emily worked together to locate the hostages, their movements swift and coordinated. The estate was a labyrinth, but their knowledge and experience guided them through the maze of rooms and corridors.

The hostages, including those from the previous incidents, were found in a secure room. They were disheveled and frightened, but unharmed. Dominic's team quickly worked to free them, their focus on ensuring their safety and well-being.

As the hostages were escorted out, Dominic and Emily prepared for the final phase of the operation: the escape. The estate's grounds were still under surveillance, and the team needed to navigate through the perimeter without being detected.

The extraction was a tense and complex operation. Dominic's team used diversionary tactics to draw attention away from their exit route, creating a window for their departure. The moonlight cast long shadows on the grounds, adding to the sense of urgency and danger.

Emily stayed close to Dominic, her presence a reassuring constant in the midst of the chaos.

The escape route was fraught with obstacles, but the team's coordination and determination ensured their progress.

As they approached the exit, Dominic's heart raced with a mix of relief and anticipation. The rescue mission had been a high-stakes operation, but they were finally on the verge of completing their objective. The sight of the waiting vehicles was a welcome relief, a sign that they were nearing the end of their ordeal.

The escape was successful, and Dominic's team made their way back to the safe house. The hostages were safely delivered, their ordeal finally over. The tension of the mission slowly began to ebb as they settled into the familiar surroundings of the safe house.

Dominic and Emily, despite their exhaustion, took a moment to reflect on the events of the night. The rescue mission had been a testament to their strength and determination, a reminder of the challenges they had faced and overcome together.

Emily's strength and bravery during the mission had been a source of immense pride for Dominic. Her involvement had been crucial, and her actions had proven her resilience and capability. Dominic's heart swelled with admiration as he looked at her, the bond between them stronger than ever.

As they debriefed and assessed the aftermath of the mission, Dominic and Emily's connection was evident. The challenges they had faced had only deepened their relationship, reinforcing their commitment and dedication to each other.

The night's events had been a crucible, testing their resolve and strength. But as they embraced, the warmth of their connection provided a sense of stability and reassurance. The future remained uncertain, but their bond was unwavering, a testament to their resilience and love.

In the quiet aftermath of the mission, Dominic and Emily faced the challenges ahead with a renewed sense of purpose and determination. The night's events had forged a stronger connection between them, a bond that would guide them through whatever came next.

Chapter Fourteen

The safe house was a quiet refuge after the chaos of the rescue mission. Nestled in a secluded part of the city, it offered both security and a much-needed respite from the high-stakes world they had been thrust into. The house was modest but well-fortified, its interior a comfortable contrast to the danger that lurked outside. It was a place where the weight of recent events could momentarily be set aside.

Dominic and Emily had arrived back from the mission hours ago, their adrenaline-fueled energy slowly giving way to exhaustion. The team had been busy tending to the hostages and reviewing the aftermath, but Dominic and Emily had found a rare moment of solitude.

They were in the living area of the safe house, a cozy space with muted lighting and simple furnishings. The room was a sanctuary of calm, a stark contrast to the tumultuous events of the night. Dominic and Emily sat together on the couch, the weight of their shared experiences hanging in the air between them.

The room was quiet except for the occasional crackle of the fireplace, its warm glow casting a soft light over the space. Dominic leaned back against the cushions, his eyes watching the flickering flames. Emily was seated beside him, her body relaxed but her mind clearly still processing the events they had endured.

Emily glanced at Dominic, her gaze thoughtful. "You've been quiet," she said softly, breaking the silence that had settled over them.

* * *

Dominic turned to face her, his expression serious but gentle. "Just thinking," he replied.

"About everything that's happened. It's been a lot to process."

Emily nodded, her eyes reflecting the warmth of the fire. "I know what you mean. The mission was intense, and it's hard to believe it's over."

Dominic's gaze softened as he studied her. The firelight highlighted the contours of her face, and he could see the exhaustion and determination that marked her features. She had been a pillar of strength throughout the ordeal, and it struck him how deeply he cared for her.

"You were incredible tonight," Dominic said, his voice filled with admiration. "You faced danger head-on, and you were a huge part of getting everyone out safely."

Emily met his gaze, a small smile touching her lips. "I couldn't have done it without you and your team. We worked well together."

Dominic's eyes held a mixture of gratitude and something deeper, something that had been simmering beneath the surface for a while. He reached out and took her hand, his touch warm and reassuring. "We made a good team. But it's not just about the mission, Emily. There's something more here that we need to talk about."

Emily's heart skipped a beat at the seriousness in his tone. She had felt a growing connection between them, but the intensity of the situation had left little room for personal reflection. Now, in this quiet moment, the opportunity for a deeper conversation had presented itself.

"What do you mean?" Emily asked, her voice barely above a whisper. She squeezed Dominic's hand gently, her eyes searching his for answers.

Dominic took a deep breath, his mind wrestling with his emotions. "I've been thinking a lot about us, about everything we've been through. This mission, the danger we faced—it's made me realize how much you mean to me."

* * *

Emily's breath caught in her throat. The weight of his words was profound, and she could feel her emotions beginning to well up. "Dominic, I—"

He interrupted her softly. "Let me finish. This isn't just about what happened tonight. It's about everything. I've been trying to understand what I'm feeling, and the truth is, I care about you more than I've ever cared about anyone."

His confession hung in the air, and Emily's heart raced. The depth of his feelings was both exhilarating and daunting. She had sensed something growing between them, but hearing him articulate it so openly was a revelation.

"I've felt the same way," Emily admitted, her voice trembling slightly. "From the moment we met, there was this undeniable connection. Everything we've been through has only made that connection stronger. I've been scared to admit it, but I can't ignore how I feel anymore."

Dominic's eyes were filled with a mixture of relief and vulnerability. He pulled her closer, his hand still holding hers tightly. "I've been scared too. Scared of how you might react, scared of what this means for us. But I can't keep pretending that my feelings for you aren't real."

Emily looked up at him, her eyes shining with emotion. "I've never felt this way about anyone before. You've shown me a side of myself I didn't know existed. You've been there for me in ways I didn't think were possible."

Dominic's heart swelled with a mixture of gratitude and love. "You've been my rock through all of this. Your strength, your courage—it's all been a beacon for me. I don't know what the future holds, but I know I want to face it with you."

Their confessions were out in the open, and the air between them was charged with a new intensity. The moments they had shared, the trials they had faced together, had forged a bond that went beyond the physical and the immediate. It was a connection rooted in shared experiences and mutual respect.

* * *

Emily leaned in closer, her forehead resting against Dominic's. The warmth of the fire and the closeness of their bodies created an intimate cocoon around them. "What does this mean for us?" she asked softly, her voice filled with both hope and uncertainty.

Dominic's fingers gently brushed against her cheek, his touch tender and reassuring. "It means we face whatever comes next together. We've proven that we can handle anything, as long as we're united. I want to build something real with you, something that goes beyond the danger and the chaos.”

Emily's eyes filled with tears of emotion. The vulnerability and honesty of their conversation had opened a new chapter in their relationship. She had always admired Dominic's strength and determination, but now she saw a different side of him—a side that was open, honest, and deeply caring.

“I want that too,” Emily said, her voice steady despite the emotions that threatened to overwhelm her. “I want to be with you, to build a life together. We've been through so much, and I believe we can handle whatever comes our way.”

Dominic's heart swelled with a sense of fulfillment. The fears and uncertainties that had plagued him were replaced by a profound sense of clarity. He leaned in and pressed a gentle kiss to her forehead, his touch a silent promise of his commitment and affection.

The kiss was tender and full of meaning, a reflection of the deep connection they shared. Emily's eyes closed as she savored the moment, her heart racing with a mixture of joy and relief. The weight of their shared experiences had brought them closer, and their confession had solidified their bond in a way that was both beautiful and profound.

As the night wore on, Dominic and Emily remained in their intimate embrace, their conversation turning to their hopes and dreams for the future. The safe house, once a symbol of their separation from the outside world, now felt like a sanctuary of possibility and promise.

* * *

Dominic's fingers traced gentle patterns on Emily's back, his touch soothing and comforting. "We've been through a lot, but we've come out stronger. I'm grateful for every moment we've shared, and I'm excited about what the future holds."

Emily smiled, her heart filled with a sense of peace and contentment. "Me too. I know we'll face challenges, but we'll face them together. That's what matters."

Their words and touches spoke of a deep and abiding connection, one that had been forged through trials and strengthened by mutual trust and respect. The intimacy they shared was more than physical; it was emotional and spiritual, a reflection of the deep bond that had developed between them.

As they sat together, wrapped in each other's arms, the future seemed both uncertain and full of promise. They had faced danger and adversity, but their love and commitment had guided them through. The night's confessions had opened a new chapter in their relationship, one that was built on honesty, vulnerability, and a shared vision for the future.

Dominic and Emily's connection was solidified in the quiet moments of the safe house, their hearts aligned and their resolve strengthened. The journey ahead would undoubtedly present new challenges, but they faced it with a renewed sense of purpose and an unwavering commitment to each other.

In the warmth of the safe house, surrounded by the soft glow of the fire and the comforting presence of one another, Dominic and Emily embraced the new chapter of their lives. The confessions of the night had deepened their bond, and they were ready to face whatever came next, united in their love and dedication.

Chapter Fifteen

The safe house, once a haven of respite, now buzzed with an air of imminent action. Dominic paced the room, his mind consumed by thoughts of retaliation. The recent kidnapping of Emily had shaken him to his core. The betrayal and danger posed by Luca Marino's allies demanded a response—a decisive and unyielding one.

The room was stark, lit only by the harsh light of overhead fixtures that accentuated the tension in Dominic's posture. Maps of the city and detailed dossiers of known associates were pinned to the walls. A large table in the center held an assortment of weapons, tactical gear, and electronic devices, all prepared for the inevitable confrontation.

Emily sat at the table, her expression resolute. Despite the trauma of her recent abduction, her demeanor was calm and focused. She had insisted on being involved in Dominic's plans for retaliation, her determination unwavering even in the face of danger.

Dominic's eyes darted to her as he reviewed the plans. "You shouldn't be here," he said, his tone edged with frustration. "This isn't a place for someone who's just been through what you have."

Emily looked up from the map, her gaze steady and unyielding. "I'm not staying on the sidelines, Dominic. You need my help. I know these people, and I can provide insights that you might not have."

Dominic's jaw tightened. He knew Emily was right; her knowledge and experience were invaluable. But the thought of her being in harm's way again was something he struggled to accept. The recent events had made him acutely aware of how much he valued her safety.

"This is different from anything we've faced before," Dominic said, his voice low and intense. "You're not just a participant; you're a target. I can't risk your life like that."

Emily stood, her stance firm and unwavering. "I understand your concern, but you can't do this alone. I've been through the worst of it, and I'm still here. I need to be part of this. It's not just about revenge; it's about making sure they can never hurt anyone else."

Dominic's eyes locked onto hers, a storm of emotions playing across his face. His anger, fear, and concern were palpable, but so was his respect for her resolve. The thought of Emily being in danger again gnawed at him, but he also knew that excluding her wasn't an option.

The atmosphere in the safe house was tense as Dominic and Emily worked through the details of their retaliation plan. The mission was to strike against those who had orchestrated Emily's kidnapping, making a statement that their actions had consequences. It was a carefully calculated response designed to dismantle the network that had threatened them.

Dominic spread out a detailed map of the city on the table, pinpointing locations that were central to Luca Marino's operations. His team gathered around, their expressions serious as they listened to his instructions. The plan was to target key players in Marino's network, disrupting their operations and sending a clear message.

Emily reviewed the plan with intense focus. She pointed out locations and potential vulnerabilities, her insights proving invaluable. Her knowledge of Marino's operations and the people involved gave Dominic and his team a strategic advantage.

"Here," Emily said, pointing to a location on the map. "This is where they're holding some of their meetings. If we hit this place, it will send a strong message. They'll know we're not backing down."

Dominic's gaze was fixed on the map, his mind racing with the implications of the plan. "We need to be precise. Any misstep could put us at risk or endanger innocent people. We strike hard, but we strike smart."

Emily nodded, her expression resolute. "We can do this. We need to show them that their actions have consequences, and we need to protect ourselves from future threats."

The discussion was meticulous, every detail scrutinized and debated. Dominic's team, seasoned professionals with experience in high-stakes operations, were fully engaged. They knew the risks involved and were prepared to act swiftly and decisively.

As the plans took shape, the tension between Dominic and Emily remained palpable. Their earlier argument had underscored the deep emotional stakes of the mission. Dominic's protective instincts clashed with Emily's determination, creating a dynamic that was both challenging and necessary.

The argument reached its peak as Dominic and Emily stepped into a quiet corner of the safe house, away from the prying eyes of the team. Dominic's frustration was evident, his anger barely contained.

"This isn't just about tactics, Emily. It's about your safety. I can't stand the thought of you being in danger again," Dominic said, his voice rising with intensity.

Emily's eyes flashed with defiance. "I get that you're worried, but this is something I have to do. I've already been through so much, and I'm not backing down now. I'm not asking for your permission; I'm asking for your support."

Dominic's hands clenched into fists, his anger a mixture of fear and helplessness. "I'm trying to protect you. You're not just another asset in this operation. You're someone I care deeply about."

Emily stepped closer, her expression softening despite her resolve. "And that's exactly why I need to be here. You care about me, and that's why I need to be part of this. I'm not going to sit back and let you handle everything alone. This is as much my fight as it is yours."

* * *

The silence that followed was heavy with unspoken emotions. Dominic's gaze softened as he looked at Emily, his heart torn between his protective instincts and his respect for her courage. He knew he couldn't keep her out of the fight—her resolve was unshakeable, and her skills were essential.

After a moment of silence, Dominic's shoulders relaxed slightly. "Alright," he said, his voice low but resigned. "If you're going to be involved, then I want you to be prepared. This isn't going to be easy, and there will be risks. But if you're with me, then we face those risks together."

Emily's expression softened with relief and gratitude. "Thank you. I promise, I'll do everything I can to support this plan and keep us both safe."

Dominic reached out and took her hand, his touch gentle and reassuring. "We need to be smart about this. Our retaliation needs to be precise, and we need to ensure that we don't leave any room for error."

As night fell, the safe house became a hive of activity. Dominic and his team prepared for the operation, their movements a mix of urgency and precision. Emily was fully integrated into the planning, her contributions crucial to the success of the mission.

Dominic's team, now accustomed to Emily's presence, worked seamlessly with her. The plan was to execute a series of coordinated strikes against key targets, disrupting Marino's operations and sending a clear message.

The first target was a warehouse on the outskirts of the city, a known hub for Marino's operations. Dominic and his team approached the location with meticulous precision, their movements coordinated and strategic.

Emily was positioned alongside Dominic, her role critical in providing intelligence and support. Her familiarity with Marino's network allowed her to identify key areas and potential threats, ensuring that the operation was executed with maximum efficiency.

The warehouse was heavily guarded, but Dominic's team was prepared. They breached the perimeter with practiced efficiency, neutralizing guards and securing key areas. The operation was a testament to their skill and coordination, their movements precise and controlled.

Emily's presence was a calming force amidst the chaos. Her tactical insights and quick thinking played a crucial role in the success of the operation. She moved with purpose, her actions a blend of confidence and resolve.

As they advanced through the warehouse, the tension was palpable. Dominic's team worked with a sense of urgency, their goal clear: dismantle Marino's operations and gather any intelligence that could further their cause. The warehouse was a labyrinth of rooms and corridors, each one a potential site for confrontation.

Emily and Dominic moved together, their actions synchronized. The strike was swift and decisive, their focus on achieving their objectives while minimizing risk. The warehouse was filled with the sounds of combat, the clash of weapons, and the occasional shout of command.

Dominic's leadership was evident as he directed his team with precision. His movements were controlled and calculated, each action aimed at achieving their goal. Emily, despite the danger, was a crucial part of the operation, her presence a source of strength and support.

As they approached the central area of the warehouse, the intensity of the operation escalated. Marino's guards were well-trained and determined, but Dominic's team was equally skilled. The confrontation was fierce, but Dominic's team was relentless.

Emily's role in the operation was crucial. Her knowledge of Marino's operations allowed her to identify key targets and potential threats. She worked alongside Dominic, her actions a testament to her bravery and skill.

The strike on the warehouse was a success, but it was just the beginning. Dominic and his team had achieved their objective, but the retaliation was far from over. The operation was a critical step in dismantling Marino's network, but there was still much work to be done.

The warehouse operation was a success, but the aftermath was a mix of exhaustion and relief. Dominic and his team returned to the safe house, their mission accomplished but the journey far from over.

Emily, despite her fatigue, was a source of strength for Dominic. Her presence and support had been invaluable throughout the operation, and their bond had only deepened as a result. The earlier argument and tension had been replaced by a shared sense of purpose and commitment.

As they debriefed and reviewed the results of the operation, Dominic and Emily shared a moment of quiet reflection. The safe house, now a symbol of their resilience, was a place where they could process the events and plan their next steps.

Dominic looked at Emily, his expression a mix of admiration and gratitude. "You were incredible tonight. Your bravery and skills made a huge difference."

Emily's eyes met his, her expression filled with a mixture of pride and exhaustion. "We did it together. It wasn't just me; it was all of us working as a team."

Dominic's gaze softened as he took her hand. "I know. And I'm grateful for your support. I couldn't have done this without you."

Emily smiled, her heart warmed by his words. "We're in this together. Whatever happens next, we'll face it as a team."

Their connection was solidified by the shared experience of the operation. The challenges they had faced and overcome had strengthened their bond, and their commitment to each other was unwavering.

As they prepared for the next phase of their journey, Dominic and Emily faced the future with a renewed sense of purpose. The retaliation was a critical step in their fight against Marino's network, but it was only the beginning.

In the quiet moments of the safe house, Dominic and Emily found solace in each other's presence. Their bond, forged through adversity and strengthened by their shared experiences, was a source of strength and comfort.

The safe house was a temporary sanctuary, but it was also a place of reflection and planning. Dominic and Emily knew that the road ahead would be challenging, but their shared commitment and determination would guide them through.

As they looked to the future, Dominic and Emily were united in their resolve to continue their fight. The retaliation had been a crucial step in their journey, but there was still much work to be done.

The events of the night had solidified their bond and reinforced their commitment to each other. The challenges they had faced had brought them closer, and their shared experiences had strengthened their connection.

In the quiet of the safe house, Dominic and Emily embraced the challenges ahead with a renewed sense of purpose. Their journey was far from over, but with their bond unbreakable and their resolve unwavering, they would survive.

Chapter Sixteen

The private mansion on the outskirts of the city was a symbol of opulence and power. Tall iron gates encircled the property, their intricate designs hinting at both wealth and security. Inside, the mansion's grandeur was reflected in its high ceilings, marble floors, and extravagant furnishings. Chandeliers cast a warm glow over the room, their light flickering off the polished surfaces and creating an atmosphere of intense anticipation.

Dominic and Emily arrived at the mansion, greeted by a sense of palpable tension that hung in the air. The purpose of their visit was critical: to form alliances with other mafia factions to consolidate power and prepare for a decisive confrontation against their common enemies. The room where the meeting was to take place was large and elegantly furnished, with a long mahogany table at its center, surrounded by high-backed chairs.

Dominic, always the picture of control and confidence, wore a dark suit that accentuated his commanding presence. Emily, equally composed, dressed in a sharp, tailored outfit that mirrored her role in the negotiations—professional yet assertive. Their combined presence was both imposing and reassuring.

As they entered the room, Dominic and Emily were met by representatives from the various factions they sought to ally with. The atmosphere was charged with a mix of curiosity, skepticism, and cautious optimism. Each faction leader had their own agenda, and the negotiations would require careful diplomacy and strategic thinking.

* * *

Dominic took his place at the head of the table, his demeanor reflecting both authority and openness. Emily stood by his side, her presence a silent but powerful testament to their partnership. The other leaders took their seats, their eyes shifting between Dominic and Emily, assessing the potential benefits and risks of the alliance.

"Thank you all for coming," Dominic began, his voice steady and commanding. "We're here to discuss a strategic alliance that will strengthen our positions and ensure that we can effectively address the threats we face. The goal is to form a unified front against those who seek to undermine us."

The room murmured with agreement and skepticism. Each leader had their own concerns and interests, and Dominic's proposal was met with both intrigue and caution. Emily observed the dynamics closely, her eyes sharp and analytical. She understood the importance of this meeting and the need to address each leader's concerns.

One of the leaders, a man known for his cunning and ruthlessness, spoke up. "We're all aware of the threat posed by Marino's network. But why should we trust you, Dominic? What guarantees do we have that this alliance will benefit us equally?"

Dominic's gaze was unwavering as he responded. "This alliance is not about dominance but about mutual benefit. We face a common enemy, and by working together, we can achieve more than we could individually. Each faction will retain its autonomy, but we will share resources and intelligence to achieve our common goals."

The room fell silent as Dominic's words sank in. The proposal was appealing, but trust was a commodity in short supply among the factions. Emily knew that the success of the meeting hinged on addressing the concerns and building trust.

The discussions became more detailed as Dominic and Emily outlined the strategic plan for the alliance. Maps and dossiers were spread out across the table, detailing key targets and objectives. The plan was designed to maximize the strengths of each faction while ensuring that their combined efforts would lead to a decisive advantage.

Emily took an active role in the planning, her expertise in intelligence and strategy proving invaluable. She addressed specific concerns raised by the faction leaders, providing detailed analyses and solutions to potential issues. Her insights helped to bridge gaps and build confidence in the alliance.

"The goal," Emily explained, "is to leverage our collective resources and knowledge to dismantle Marino's operations. We need to coordinate our efforts and ensure that we're targeting their key assets and weaknesses."

One of the leaders, a woman known for her strategic acumen, nodded in agreement. "I see the potential in this plan. But how do we ensure that we're not exposing ourselves to greater risk? Marino's network is extensive and dangerous."

Emily met her gaze steadily. "We'll implement a phased approach, starting with intelligence gathering and targeted strikes. Each faction will be responsible for specific tasks, and we'll coordinate our actions to minimize risk and maximize impact."

The leaders listened attentively as Emily spoke, her confidence and expertise making a strong impression. Dominic observed the interactions with a mixture of satisfaction and concern. The success of the alliance depended on the ability to manage complex relationships and navigate the intricate web of mafia politics.

As the strategic planning continued, Dominic and Emily worked to build trust and rapport with the faction leaders. They made it clear that the alliance was based on mutual benefit and shared goals, emphasizing the importance of cooperation and communication.

Dominic addressed the leaders individually, answering questions and addressing concerns. His approach was direct and transparent, aimed at demonstrating his commitment to the alliance and his respect for the autonomy of each faction.

Emily played a crucial role in facilitating these interactions, her diplomatic skills and tactical insights helping to bridge gaps and resolve conflicts. Her ability to articulate the benefits of the alliance and address specific concerns was instrumental in gaining the leaders' trust.

In private conversations, Dominic and Emily discussed their strategy and addressed any lingering doubts. They knew that the success of the alliance hinged on their ability to manage relationships and maintain a unified front.

"This is a delicate situation," Emily said during one of their discussions. "We need to be cautious and ensure that we're addressing the concerns of each faction. Trust is essential, and we need to be prepared for any challenges that may arise."

Dominic nodded in agreement. "I understand. We've made progress, but there's still much work to be done. The key is to maintain open communication and be responsive to any issues that arise."

Throughout the meeting, the chemistry between Dominic and Emily was undeniable. Their partnership was a blend of professionalism and personal connection, their interactions seamless and effective. Their ability to work together was a testament to their mutual respect and understanding.

As they reviewed the strategic plan and addressed the leaders' concerns, their teamwork was evident. Dominic's authoritative presence and Emily's analytical skills complemented each other, creating a dynamic that was both powerful and effective.

During breaks in the meeting, Dominic and Emily shared quiet moments of reflection, their conversations revealing the depth of their connection. They discussed the progress of the negotiations, their thoughts on the leaders' reactions, and their plans for the next steps.

Emily looked at Dominic with a mixture of admiration and determination. "We're making progress, but we need to stay focused. This alliance is crucial, and we need to ensure that we're addressing any issues that arise."

Dominic met her gaze with a mixture of respect and concern. "I know.

Your insights have been invaluable, and your ability to navigate these negotiations has made a significant difference. I'm grateful for your support."

Emily's eyes softened with appreciation. "We're in this together. We've faced challenges before, and we'll face them again. But as long as we work together, we'll succeed."

As the meeting concluded, Dominic and Emily felt a sense of accomplishment. The groundwork for the alliance had been laid, and the strategic plan was set. The leaders had agreed to the terms, and the collaboration was poised to begin.

The next steps involved implementing the plan and coordinating actions among the factions. Dominic and Emily would play a central role in overseeing the operations and ensuring that the alliance remained focused and effective.

As they left the mansion, Dominic and Emily shared a moment of quiet reflection. The day had been demanding, but the results were promising. Their partnership had proven to be a powerful force, and their connection had only deepened.

Dominic looked at Emily with a mixture of pride and gratitude. "We've made significant progress today. Your contributions have been invaluable, and I'm grateful for your support."

Emily smiled, her eyes reflecting a sense of accomplishment. "We've achieved a lot, but there's still much work to be done. We need to stay focused and ensure that our plan is executed effectively."

Dominic nodded in agreement. "Absolutely. This is just the beginning. We've built a strong foundation, and now we need to build on it and see our plan through to success."

As they drove away from the mansion, the city lights glittered in the distance, a symbol of the challenges and opportunities that lay ahead. Dominic and Emily were united in their resolve, their partnership a testament to their strength and determination.

* * *

The alliance was a critical step in their journey, and their combined efforts would shape the future. With their bond solidified and their goals clear, Dominic and Emily faced the future with a renewed sense of purpose and commitment. The road ahead was uncertain, but they were prepared to face it together, their alliance a beacon of hope and strength in the face of adversity.

Chapter Seventeen

The night was cloaked in darkness, punctuated only by the occasional flash of distant lightning. The rain fell steadily, creating a rhythmic drumming on the rooftops and streets. The city seemed to hold its breath, aware of the monumental confrontation about to unfold. Dominic and Emily had spent weeks meticulously planning for this night, the culmination of their efforts against Marino's network.

The battleground was an abandoned warehouse on the outskirts of the city, a desolate place that had seen better days. Once a thriving hub of industrial activity, it now stood in stark contrast to its former glory. Broken windows, rusted metal beams, and scattered debris littered the area. The warehouse's large, cavernous interior was dimly lit by sporadic flickers of emergency lights, casting eerie shadows that danced across the walls.

Dominic's team was already on-site, their vehicles strategically positioned around the perimeter. Each man and woman was prepared for the imminent battle, armed and vigilant. Emily, now fully integrated into Dominic's world, was with him, her presence a crucial asset in the fight.

The plan was simple yet daring: launch a coordinated assault to cripple Marino's operations and eliminate his top enforcers. The stakes were high, and the risks were enormous. This battle would determine not only their immediate survival but also the future of their struggle against the criminal empire.

* * *

Dominic and Emily stood together in the control room, a makeshift command center set up in one corner of the warehouse. Monitors displayed live feeds from various cameras set up around the area, showing the movements of Marino's men and the layout of the warehouse. The air was thick with anticipation and the scent of rain soaked concrete.

Dominic's eyes were steely with focus. He wore tactical gear that accentuated his imposing figure, and his expression was a blend of determination and controlled aggression. Emily, equally prepared, adjusted her gear and reviewed her own set of equipment—a combination of combat readiness and tech gadgets that had become essential to her role.

"Are we ready?" Dominic's voice cut through the tension like a knife.

Emily nodded, her expression resolute. "All systems are go. We've got eyes on every entrance, and our team is in position."

Dominic glanced at the monitors, assessing the situation. "Good. Let's go over the plan one more time. We'll hit them from multiple angles, focusing on their command structure first. We need to disrupt their coordination and create confusion."

Emily's eyes met his with a shared understanding. "I'll take the east side with my team. We'll use the element of surprise to our advantage."

Dominic's gaze softened slightly, a rare moment of vulnerability. "Be careful out there. We've come too far to let anything go wrong now."

Emily reached out and touched his arm briefly, a gesture of reassurance. "You too. We're in this together."

With a final nod, Dominic turned to his team, giving them a series of hand signals and verbal cues that set the operation into motion. The warehouse was about to become a battlefield, and every second counted.

The first wave of attacks came swiftly and with precision. Emily led her team through a side entrance, her movements fluid and decisive.

The sound of gunfire and explosions reverberated through the warehouse as Dominic's forces engaged Marino's men in a chaotic dance of violence.

Emily moved with purpose, her instincts sharp and her combat skills on full display. She ducked behind cover, firing her weapon with calculated accuracy. Her tactical training and experience made her a formidable opponent, and her presence on the battlefield was a testament to her growth since joining Dominic's world.

Dominic, meanwhile, was at the forefront of the assault. His leadership and combat prowess were evident as he orchestrated the attack with precision. His team followed his lead, moving in sync and executing their tactics flawlessly.

The warehouse became a maelstrom of gunfire, shouting, and chaos. The dim lighting and shadowy corners added to the sense of disorientation, making every corner a potential danger. Dominic and Emily fought side by side, their movements a synchronized blend of aggression and strategy.

As the battle raged on, Emily found herself facing off against some of Marino's top enforcers. The confrontation was intense, a brutal clash of skill and determination. Emily's training and resourcefulness were put to the test as she engaged in close-quarters combat, her every move a calculated response to her opponents' attacks.

Dominic was a force of nature, his presence commanding and his actions decisive. He led his team with unwavering confidence, his focus on the objective clear despite the chaos surrounding him. His leadership was a critical factor in the success of the operation, and his strategic decisions ensured that they maintained the upper hand.

The turning point in the battle came when Dominic and Emily's coordinated attack reached Marino's inner sanctum—a fortified area within the warehouse where Marino and his top lieutenants were holed up. The room was heavily guarded, and the fighting was particularly fierce.

* * *

Dominic and Emily breached the room with a combination of tactical precision and brute force. The guards were overwhelmed by the sheer intensity of the assault, their defenses crumbling under the relentless pressure. The final showdown with Marino's inner circle was a brutal and decisive clash.

Emily fought with a fierce determination, her movements a blur of efficiency as she took down her opponents. Dominic, equally relentless, engaged Marino's top enforcers with a combination of strategic brilliance and raw power. The intensity of the battle reached its peak as they pushed through the defenses and confronted Marino himself.

The confrontation with Marino was personal and intense. Marino, a formidable and ruthless adversary, was a stark contrast to Dominic's calculated aggression. The two men clashed with a ferocity that reflected their long-standing animosity and the stakes of the battle.

The fight was a brutal exchange of blows and tactics, each man testing the other's limits. Dominic's strength and skill were matched by Marino's cunning and brutality, creating a high-stakes battle that was as much about willpower as it was about physical prowess.

Emily, despite being engaged in her own battle, kept a close watch on Dominic. Her concern for him was evident as she fought off Marino's remaining enforcers, her every move a testament to her commitment to their mission.

The battle reached its climax as Dominic and Marino faced off in a final, decisive confrontation. The warehouse was filled with the sounds of battle, but in this moment, everything else seemed to fade away. The two men fought with a primal intensity, their every movement a reflection of their deep-seated conflict.

In a final, brutal exchange, Dominic gained the upper hand. His strength and determination proved decisive as he overpowered Marino, delivering the blows that ended the fight. Marino fell, defeated and broken, his reign of terror coming to an end.

The warehouse fell silent as the last of Marino's men were either

Bound By Danger

captured or fled. The victory was hard-earned, and the cost was evident in the aftermath. Dominic's team was battered and bruised, their victory marred by the toll of the battle.

Emily, despite her exhaustion and injuries, approached Dominic with a mixture of relief and concern. She could see the strain in his eyes, the weight of the battle taking its toll. The warehouse, once a symbol of their struggle, now stood as a testament to their hard-fought victory.

Dominic looked at Emily, his expression a mixture of triumph and weariness. "We did it. Marino's gone, and his network is shattered."

Emily nodded, her voice weary but resolute. "We won, but the cost was high. We need to take care of the wounded and make sure that we're prepared for whatever comes next."

Dominic's gaze softened as he looked at Emily. "You were incredible out there. Your bravery and skill made all the difference."

Emily's eyes met his with a mixture of gratitude and fatigue. "We did it together. That's what matters."

As they took stock of the aftermath, the reality of their victory began to sink in. The battle was over, but the fight was far from finished. The remnants of Marino's network still posed a threat, and the road ahead would be challenging.

Dominic and Emily stood together in the midst of the wreckage; their bond strengthened by the shared experience. The victory was a testament to their strength and determination, but it also highlighted the sacrifices they had made along the way.

In the quiet moments after the battle, Dominic and Emily reflected on the events that had transpired. The warehouse, now a scene of devastation, was a stark reminder of the cost of their victory. The sense of relief was tempered by the knowledge of the challenges that lay ahead.

Dominic and Emily shared a moment of solitude amidst the chaos, their connection a source of comfort and strength. They knew that the road ahead would be difficult, but their shared experiences and unwavering commitment to each other provided a sense of hope.

As they prepared to leave the warehouse, Dominic looked at Emily with a mixture of pride and resolve. "We've accomplished a lot tonight, but there's still much work to be done. We need to rebuild and prepare for what comes next."

Emily nodded, her expression determined. "We'll face whatever comes together. We've proven that we can overcome anything as long as we're united."

The night was still young, and the city awaited their next move. Dominic and Emily were ready to face the future, their bond and their victory a testament to their strength and resilience. The battle was over, but their journey was far from complete. As they walked away from the warehouse, they did so with a renewed sense of purpose and a deepened connection.

Chapter Eighteen

The safe house, nestled in a secluded part of the city, was a stark contrast to the chaos of the recent battle. It was a haven of calm, designed to provide sanctuary and respite from the turmoil of their lives. The interior was spacious and comfortable, with large windows offering a view of the tranquil surroundings. Soft, ambient light filled the rooms, creating a soothing atmosphere.

Dominic and Emily arrived at the safe house, their bodies and spirits weighed down by the aftermath of the intense conflict. The once pristine interior now bore signs of their recent ordeal—scattered equipment, makeshift medical supplies, and the occasional sign of the chaos that had unfolded.

The safe house was equipped with everything they needed to recover: medical supplies, comfortable living spaces, and the necessary amenities to allow them to heal both physically and emotionally. As Dominic and Emily stepped inside, they were greeted by the familiar scent of antiseptic and the soft hum of a ventilation system.

Dominic, though visibly exhausted, moved with a purposeful energy. He immediately began to assess the condition of the safe house and ensure that everything was in order. Emily, equally weary, took a moment to absorb the quietude, appreciating the sanctuary that the safe house represented.

Dominic and Emily had both sustained injuries during the battle. Dominic's wounds were primarily superficial—scratches and bruises that would heal with time. Emily's injuries were more significant, including a deep gash on her side and a concussion from a particularly harsh blow. The immediate priority was to tend to their wounds and begin the process of recovery.

Emily made her way to the medical room, a space set up for treating injuries and providing comfort. The room was equipped with an assortment of medical supplies, including bandages, antiseptics, and pain relief medications. She began to carefully tend to her own wounds, her movements deliberate and focused despite her fatigue.

Dominic entered the room, his eyes scanning the space with a mix of concern and practicality. He took a seat at a nearby table and began to clean and dress his own wounds. The silence between them was heavy, filled with the weight of their shared experiences.

Emily looked up from her work, her expression a mixture of determination and vulnerability. "We need to get these injuries treated properly. We can't afford to let them get worse."

Dominic nodded, his gaze shifting from his own wounds to Emily's. "I'll handle the medical supplies. You focus on getting yourself patched up."

Emily gave a small, appreciative smile. "Thanks. I could use some help."

As they worked together in the quiet room, Dominic and Emily began to reflect on their journey. The battle had been a culmination of their efforts, but the emotional and psychological toll was just beginning to be felt. The healing process was as much about addressing their internal wounds as it was about their physical injuries.

Dominic carefully applied a bandage to Emily's side, his touch gentle despite his usual commanding demeanor. "You were incredible out there. I don't know if I've ever seen anyone fight with the same intensity and skill."

Emily winced slightly as the bandage was secured but managed a wry smile. "You weren't too bad yourself. We make a pretty good team, don't we?"

Dominic's eyes met hers, his expression softening. "Yeah, we do. But it's not just about fighting. It's about everything we've been through together—how we've changed and grown."

Emily's gaze was thoughtful as she considered his words. "It's been a hell of a journey. I've learned so much about myself and about us. It's not just about surviving the battles; it's about what we've become in the process."

Dominic's fingers lingered on the bandage as he spoke, his voice thoughtful. "I never imagined that I'd find someone who could challenge me, support me, and be my equal in every way. You've done all that and more."

Emily's eyes met his with a mixture of gratitude and tenderness. "I never thought I'd find someone who could understand me like you do.

We've been through so much, and it's changed us. For the better, I think."

Dominic nodded, his gaze unwavering. "Yeah. It's changed us both. And as much as we've fought against the world, we've also found something worth fighting for."

Emily's expression softened, her eyes reflecting a deep emotional connection. "We have. We've found each other. And that's something I wouldn't trade for anything."

As they continued to tend to their wounds, the intimacy of the moment allowed their relationship to deepen further. The vulnerability they shared in their recovery process brought them closer together, revealing layers of their connection that had been forged through their shared experiences.

Dominic finished bandaging Emily's injuries and took a moment to sit beside her, their proximity allowing them to share a quiet, reflective moment. Emily leaned back against the wall, her gaze distant yet thoughtful.

* * *

Dominic's voice broke the silence, gentle and sincere. "We've faced so much together. It's hard to believe how far we've come. And now, with everything that's happened, I want to make sure we're not just moving forward in the same fight but also in our lives together."

Emily turned to face him, her eyes filled with a mixture of hope and resolve. "I want that too. I want us to find a way to be more than just survivors of this fight. I want us to build something together— something that's ours."

Dominic's expression softened as he reached out to touch her hand. "We will. We'll find a way to move forward and create a life together. We've faced the worst, and we've come out stronger. I believe we can build something lasting."

Emily's eyes met his with a mixture of determination and affection. "I believe that too. We've already proven that we're stronger together. Now it's about finding our way forward and building on that strength."

The connection between them was palpable, a testament to the depth of their bond. They had fought together, healed together, and now they faced the future with a shared commitment and a renewed sense of purpose.

As the night wore on, Dominic and Emily settled into a comfortable routine of recovery. They worked together to ensure that their wounds were properly treated, taking turns to rest and recuperate. The safe house provided a refuge from the outside world, allowing them to focus on their healing and their relationship.

In the quiet moments, they talked about their hopes and dreams for the future. They discussed their plans, their fears, and their aspirations. The conversations were intimate and revealing, allowing them to explore the depth of their connection and their shared vision for what lay ahead.

Dominic and Emily also took time to reflect on the lessons they had learned throughout their journey. They spoke about their personal growth, their evolving relationship, and the ways in which they had changed. The reflections were a mixture of introspection and optimism, marking a significant step in their emotional healing.

As dawn approached, the first light of morning began to filter through the windows of the safe house. Dominic and Emily sat together, their hands intertwined, a symbol of their shared strength and commitment.

Dominic looked at Emily with a mixture of gratitude and affection. "We've come a long way. And despite everything we've been through, I'm grateful for the journey we've shared."

Emily's eyes were warm as she responded. "Me too. We've faced challenges and overcome them. And now, we have the chance to build something new together."

The morning light cast a soft glow over the room, illuminating the promise of a new beginning. Dominic and Emily were ready to face the future, their bond strengthened by their shared experiences and their commitment to each other.

As they prepared to move forward, they did so with a sense of hope and determination. The road ahead would be challenging, but they were united in their resolve to build a future together. The healing process had deepened their connection, and their journey was far from over.

Dominic and Emily stood together, ready to face whatever came next. Their relationship had evolved through their trials, and their shared strength and commitment would guide them as they forged their path forward. The safe house had been a sanctuary of healing, and now they were prepared to embrace the next chapter of their lives, together.

Chapter Nineteen

The safe house, now a symbol of their triumph and recovery, was bathed in the soft light of a new morning. The previous night had been a quiet respite, filled with the subtle hum of the air conditioner and the occasional rustle of movement. Today, however, the calm was underscored by an undercurrent of tension—an unspoken decision that loomed over Dominic and Emily.

The safe house had become a temporary refuge, a place where they could catch their breath and regroup. Its interior, while still functional and comfortable, felt like a cocoon from which they would soon have to emerge. The walls, adorned with simple decor, seemed to close in around them, amplifying the gravity of the conversation they were about to have.

Dominic and Emily sat across from each other at the kitchen table, the space around them cluttered with remnants of their recovery—bandages, medical supplies, and half-empty mugs of coffee. The morning light streamed through the large windows, casting a warm glow that did little to dispel the weight of their impending discussion.

The battle had left its mark on both of them, not just physically but emotionally as well. Dominic had fought hard to protect Emily and to dismantle Marino's empire. For Emily, the choice was more profound —she had to decide whether to continue in this dangerous world or to carve out a different path for herself.

Emily's gaze was fixed on the half-empty coffee cup in front of her, her fingers tracing its rim absentmindedly. She was lost in thought, her mind wrestling with the enormity of the decision she faced. Dominic, seated across from her, was acutely aware of her internal struggle.

His usual composure was replaced by a quiet, concerned demeanor as he observed her.

Dominic's voice broke the silence, gentle but firm. "Emily, we need to talk about what happens next. I know this world is not what you planned for yourself. You've been through so much, and I want you to be sure about what you're choosing."

Emily's eyes met his, revealing the uncertainty and conflict she felt. "I've been thinking about it a lot. I've seen what this life demands, and I know the risks involved. It's not just about fighting anymore; it's about living with the constant danger and uncertainty."

Dominic's expression softened, a mix of concern and respect in his eyes. "I understand that. This life is not easy, and it's not something I would ever want to force on you. I want you to make this decision for yourself, not out of obligation or guilt."

Emily took a deep breath, her mind racing through their recent experiences. She thought about the battles they had fought, the trust they had built, and the future they had envisioned together. The reality of Dominic's world was daunting, but it was also intertwined with the life she had come to embrace.

Emily's voice was steady, though tinged with emotion. "I've seen the danger and the chaos, but I've also seen the purpose and the passion behind it. You've shown me a side of this world that's not just about power and violence—it's about fighting for something greater."

Dominic's gaze remained fixed on her, his eyes reflecting a deep, genuine concern. "I don't want you to feel trapped. This is a dangerous life, and it's not one that everyone can handle. I've seen too many people get hurt or lose themselves in this world."

Emily's expression was thoughtful, her eyes searching Dominic's face for answers. "I've thought about what my life would be like if I walked away. And while there's a part of me that wants a simpler, safer life, there's also a part of me that's found something valuable in this fight. It's not just about being with you; it's about what we stand for."

Dominic's voice was filled with a mixture of hope and apprehension. "You don't have to make any decisions right away. We can take our time and figure out what's best for us. But I need to know where you stand, so I can understand how to move forward."

Emily reached out and took Dominic's hand, her touch a blend of reassurance and resolve. "I've already made my decision. I've seen what we can achieve together, and I believe in what we're doing. I want to stay. I want to be part of this world, with all its challenges and risks. But I need to be sure that we're making this choice together, with full understanding of what it means."

Dominic's eyes softened, a mixture of relief and admiration in his gaze. "Are you sure? This life is demanding, and it's not going to get any easier. But if you're committed, I'm with you every step of the way."

Emily nodded, her voice steady and resolute. "I'm sure. I know there will be risks, but I'm ready to face them. I want to be with you, and I want to fight for what we believe in. Together."

The decision had been made, and with it came a renewed sense of purpose and commitment. The tension that had hung over them seemed to dissipate, replaced by a shared determination to face the future together.

Dominic's expression was a mixture of relief and gratitude. "Thank you for being honest and for making this decision. I know it wasn't easy, and I appreciate your commitment. We'll face whatever comes next together, and we'll find a way to make it work."

Emily's eyes met his with a blend of affection and determination. "I'm ready for whatever comes our way. We've faced so much already, and I believe we can handle whatever challenges lie ahead."

Dominic's gaze softened as he reached out to embrace Emily. The hug was a comforting reminder of their bond, a symbol of their shared strength and resolve. They held each other tightly, finding solace in their connection and the knowledge that they were facing the future as a united front.

As they broke the embrace, Dominic looked at Emily with a newfound sense of optimism. "We've got a lot of work ahead of us. We need to rebuild and plan for the future. But we'll do it together, and we'll make sure that we're prepared for whatever comes next."

Emily nodded, her expression one of determined resolve. "We will. We'll face the challenges and build the future we want. And we'll do it with the understanding that we're in this together."

With their decision made, Dominic and Emily began to focus on the tasks that lay ahead. The immediate concern was to stabilize their operations and ensure that they were prepared for any remaining threats. The safe house would remain a crucial part of their strategy, providing a base of operations as they navigated the complexities of their world.

Emily's commitment to Dominic's world brought a new sense of purpose to their efforts. She was determined to make a difference and to contribute to their shared goals. Her presence was a source of strength and inspiration for Dominic, who valued her dedication and resilience.

As they worked together to address the aftermath of their recent battles, Dominic and Emily found themselves growing even closer. Their shared experiences had forged a deep bond, and their commitment to each other was unwavering.

The future was still uncertain, but with their decision made, Dominic and Emily were ready to face it with a sense of purpose and determination. They were prepared to confront the challenges ahead and to build a life together that was grounded in their shared values and goals.

Their journey was far from over, but they faced it with renewed confidence and a deepened connection. The decision to stay and fight together marked a new chapter in their lives, one that would be defined by their strength, their love, and their commitment to each other.

As they prepared to move forward, Dominic and Emily did so with a sense of hope and optimism. They were ready to embrace the future, whatever it might hold, and to build a life together that was meaningful and fulfilling. The decision had been made, and they were ready to face the challenges and opportunities that lay ahead, united in their resolve and their love.

Chapter Twenty

Months had passed since Emily had made the momentous decision to stay in Dominic's world. The safe house, once a symbol of their immediate refuge, had transformed into a home—a place where they had crafted a life together amidst the complexities of their existence. The once sterile and functional space was now warm and inviting, decorated with personal touches that spoke to their shared journey.

Dominic and Emily had created a sanctuary from the chaos that had surrounded them. The interior of their home was a blend of comfort and practicality. The walls were adorned with photographs of their shared moments—both mundane and extraordinary. The living room, with its plush sofas and soft lighting, was a testament to the life they had built together. It was a place where they could unwind and find solace from the demands of their world.

The kitchen, a hub of their domestic life, was a blend of functionality and warmth. It was here that they shared their meals, their conversations, and their daily routines. The scent of freshly brewed coffee and home-cooked meals was a comforting reminder of their settled life, even as they continued to navigate the complexities of their existence.

Outside, the garden was a vibrant oasis, a space where they could escape the pressures of their lives. Lush greenery and blooming flowers created a tranquil environment, a stark contrast to the violence and turmoil that had once defined their world. It was a place where they could find peace and reflect on their journey.

* * *

One sunny afternoon, Dominic and Emily were enjoying a rare moment of relaxation in their garden. The warmth of the sun and the gentle rustling of leaves created a serene atmosphere, allowing them to momentarily forget the challenges that lay beyond their sanctuary.

Dominic was lounging in a hammock, a book resting on his chest, while Emily was seated at a nearby table, working on her laptop. The peacefulness of the garden was punctuated by the occasional chirp of birds and the distant hum of traffic. It was a moment of calm that they both cherished.

Their tranquility was abruptly interrupted by the sound of their secure phone ringing—a signal that their routine was about to be disrupted. Dominic's eyes flickered open, and he sat up, his relaxed demeanor replaced by a look of concentration. He reached for the phone, glancing at Emily, who had already closed her laptop and was watching him with a mixture of curiosity and concern.

"Looks like we've got a situation," Dominic said, his tone serious as he answered the call. His expression was a blend of focus and determination, reflecting the gravity of the message he had received.

Emily joined him, her gaze steady as she listened to the details of the situation. "What's going on?" she asked, her voice calm despite the sudden shift in their mood.

Dominic's expression was tense as he relayed the information. "There's a new threat. It seems that one of our old adversaries has resurfaced, and they're looking to settle scores. We need to act quickly to address this."

Emily's eyes met Dominic's, a steely resolve in her gaze. "We'll handle it. What's the plan?"

Dominic nodded; his expression resolute. "We need to gather intel and strategize. We can't afford to underestimate this threat."

The following days were a whirlwind of activity as Dominic and Emily prepared for the new challenge. They mobilized their resources, contacting allies and gathering information. The threat was significant, and it required a coordinated effort to address it effectively.

Dominic and Emily worked seamlessly together, their bond and understanding evident in their interactions. They strategized, planned, and executed their tasks with precision. The challenge brought them closer, as they relied on each other's strengths and supported one another through the process.

As they delved into the details of the threat, they uncovered a complex web of deception and manipulation. Their adversary, a former associate with a vendetta, had been plotting a series of attacks designed to destabilize their operations and undermine their progress.

Emily's expertise in technology and intelligence played a crucial role in unraveling the threat. She worked tirelessly, analyzing data and uncovering key information that would guide their response. Her dedication and skill were instrumental in devising a strategy to counter the threat effectively.

Dominic's leadership and strategic acumen were equally vital. He coordinated their efforts, making critical decisions and ensuring that their response was both swift and effective. His ability to remain calm under pressure and his unwavering commitment to their cause were key factors in navigating the challenge.

The climax of their response came on a rainy night, the weather adding a layer of intensity to their operation. Dominic and Emily, along with their team, were ready to confront the threat head-on. The atmosphere was charged with anticipation as they prepared for the confrontation.

The location was a warehouse on the outskirts of the city, a place that had been identified as the site of their adversary's operations. The rain poured down in heavy sheets, creating a backdrop of noise and obscurity. The team moved with purpose; their movements synchronized as they approached the warehouse.

Dominic and Emily took the lead, their presence commanding attention. Dominic's gaze was focused, his mind calculating the best approach. Emily, by his side, was equally determined, her readiness to face the challenge evident in her stance.

As they entered the warehouse, the scene that unfolded was both chaotic and tense. The adversary's operatives were prepared for a confrontation, and the ensuing battle was fierce. Dominic and Emily fought with a combination of skill and determination, their actions reflecting the bond and unity they had forged.

Emily's fighting prowess was on full display as she maneuvered through the warehouse, her movements precise and powerful. Dominic, equally adept, fought alongside her, their coordination seamless. The intensity of the battle underscored their strength as a team, their ability to face adversity together evident in every move they made.

Despite the challenges they faced, Dominic and Emily managed to overcome their adversaries, neutralizing the threat and securing their position. The warehouse, once a site of danger, was now a symbol of their victory and resilience.

As the battle concluded and the dust settled, Dominic and Emily took a moment to regroup and assess the situation. The rain continued to fall outside, its rhythm a soothing counterpoint to the intensity of the confrontation.

Dominic's gaze met Emily's, a mixture of relief and admiration in his eyes. "We did it. We faced the threat and came out on top."

Emily's expression was one of quiet satisfaction, her resolve unwavering. "We did. It was a tough fight, but we handled it well. Our teamwork made all the difference."

Dominic reached out, taking Emily's hand in his. The touch was a gesture of reassurance and connection, a reminder of the bond that had carried them through the challenge. "I couldn't have done it without you. Your skills and dedication were crucial."

Emily's eyes softened as she returned his gesture. "And I couldn't have done it without you. Your leadership and strength made all the difference."

* * *

The sense of accomplishment was palpable, a testament to their unity and strength as a couple. They had faced a significant challenge and emerged victorious, their bond strengthened by the experience.

As they left the warehouse and returned to their safe house, the sense of peace and contentment was a welcome relief. The rain had eased to a light drizzle, and the city's lights twinkled in the distance—a reminder of the world they had worked so hard to protect.

Back at their home, Dominic and Emily settled into a quiet evening, their exhaustion tempered by a sense of fulfillment. The garden, now bathed in the soft glow of evening light, provided a serene backdrop for their reflection.

Dominic and Emily sat together on the porch, the comfortable chairs a symbol of their shared life. The evening was calm, the air crisp and fresh after the rain. They took a moment to appreciate the tranquility, their gazes fixed on the horizon.

Dominic's voice broke the silence, soft and contemplative. "We've come a long way. We've faced so many challenges, but we've built something real and lasting."

Emily's gaze was thoughtful as she responded. "We have. And through it all, we've found a way to make our lives meaningful. We've faced the dangers, and we've come out stronger."

Dominic's expression was one of contentment as he reached for Emily's hand. "We've built a life together, one that's grounded in our shared values and commitment. I'm grateful for everything we've accomplished."

Emily's eyes met his with a mixture of love and determination. "I am too. We've created something special, and I believe we can continue to build on that. The future is ours to shape."

The moment was a quiet celebration of their journey, a reflection on their accomplishments and the life they had built together. Their bond, forged through adversity and strengthened by their shared experiences, was a testament to their love and commitment.

As they looked toward the future, Dominic and Emily did so with a sense of optimism and hope.

They had faced challenges and emerged victorious, their relationship deepened by their experiences. The road ahead was filled with possibilities, and they were ready to embrace it with confidence and determination.

Their shared life was a testament to their strength as a couple, their ability to face adversity together, and their commitment to building a future that was grounded in their love and values. The journey had been tumultuous, but it had led them to a place of peace and contentment—a place where they could look forward to their future with hope and excitement.

As the evening drew to a close, Dominic and Emily found solace in each other's presence. The challenges they had faced had only strengthened their bond, and they were ready to face whatever came next, united in their love and their shared vision for the future. The sense of peace and contentment that enveloped them was a testament to their journey—a journey that had brought them closer and had shaped their lives in ways they had never imagined.

Epilogue

The city skyline shimmered under the early morning sun, casting a golden hue over the streets that had once been battlegrounds. A new day dawned, marking a chapter of peace after the turmoil that had defined Dominic and Emily's journey. Their world, once fraught with danger and deception, had transformed into a landscape of hope and renewal.

In the heart of their safe house, now fully integrated into their lives, Dominic and Emily enjoyed a quiet morning together. The living space, adorned with personal touches and mementos from their shared experiences, reflected their newfound sense of stability and contentment. The chaos of their past seemed distant, replaced by the simple pleasures of their domestic life.

Emily stood by the kitchen counter, her hands busy preparing breakfast. The aroma of freshly brewed coffee and sizzling bacon filled the air, a comforting reminder of their routine. Dominic, relaxed in casual attire, watched her with a smile. The easy camaraderie and affection between them spoke volumes about their deepened bond.

As they sat down to breakfast, the conversation flowed effortlessly, a blend of playful banter and heartfelt reflections. They discussed their plans for the day, from meetings with allies to moments of relaxation. Their interactions were marked by a sense of ease and understanding, a testament to the strength of their relationship.

With the morning routine complete, Dominic and Emily ventured outside. The garden, now in full bloom, was a vibrant testament to their efforts. They had cultivated not just plants, but a space of tranquility—a sanctuary from the demands of their world. The garden had become a symbol of their resilience and their commitment to building a future together.

As they walked through the garden, hand in hand, Dominic's gaze softened. "It's amazing how much has changed. I never imagined we'd come this far."

Emily squeezed his hand gently. "Neither did I. But we've built something beautiful out of everything we've faced. Our journey has made us stronger."

Dominic nodded, his eyes reflecting the warmth of the morning sun. "We've faced so much together—challenges, threats, and uncertainties. But we've emerged stronger, and we've built a life that's grounded in our love and commitment."

Emily's gaze was thoughtful as she looked around the garden. "We have. And now, we can focus on the future we've dreamed of. We've worked hard to get here, and we deserve this moment of peace."

Their conversation was interrupted by the sound of a car pulling up the driveway. Dominic's expression shifted to one of curiosity, while Emily's eyes sparkled with intrigue. The arrival of visitors was a reminder of their continued role in the world they had navigated so skillfully.

As they approached the driveway, they were greeted by familiar faces —friends and allies who had stood by them throughout their journey. The gathering was a celebration of their triumphs and their commitment to a shared vision. The atmosphere was one of camaraderie and joy, a fitting tribute to the resilience and unity that had defined their path.

The day unfolded with laughter, stories, and reflections on their journey. The gathering was not just a celebration of their victory, but also a testament to the relationships they had forged and the support they had received. It was a reminder of the importance of community and the strength that came from standing together.

As the sun dipped below the horizon, Dominic and Emily found a quiet moment away from the festivities. The sky was painted with hues of pink and orange, creating a serene backdrop for their reflections. They stood together, their arms wrapped around each other, their gazes fixed on the beauty of the evening.

Dominic's voice was soft and filled with gratitude. "We've come so far, and we've achieved so much. But it's the journey we've shared that means the most to me."

Emily's eyes were filled with warmth as she looked at him. "And to me. Our journey has been one of growth and transformation. We've faced the darkest moments and emerged stronger, together."

Dominic's expression was one of deep contentment. "Here's to the future—a future built on the strength of our love and the resilience we've shown. Whatever comes next, I know we'll face it together."

Emily nodded, her gaze steady. "Whatever comes next, we'll face it with the same courage and commitment that has brought us here. We've built a life worth fighting for, and we'll continue to cherish and protect it."

As they stood together, enveloped in the quiet beauty of the evening, they felt a profound sense of peace. The trials and tribulations of their past had shaped their journey, but they had emerged with a renewed sense of purpose and a deepened connection. Their story, marked by love, courage, and resilience, had reached a moment of tranquility—a moment to savor and cherish as they looked forward to the future they would build together.